Blood Rid‹

Book One: I

Order this book online at www.trafford.com
or email orders@trafford.com

Most Trafford titles are also available at major online book retailers.

© Copyright 2009 Elizabeth Gulley.
Laurent Laveder, cover illustration (http://www.pixheaven.net)

Note for Librarians: A cataloguing record for this book is available from Library
and Archives Canada at www.collectionscanada.ca/amicus/index-e.html

Printed in Victoria, BC, Canada.

ISBN: 978-1-4269-0233-8

*We at Trafford believe that it is the responsibility of us all, as both individuals
and corporations, to make choices that are environmentally and socially sound.
You, in turn, are supporting this responsible conduct each time you purchase a
Trafford book, or make use of our publishing services. To find out how you are
helping, please visit www.trafford.com/responsiblepublishing.html*

*Our mission is to efficiently provide the world's finest, most comprehensive
book publishing service, enabling every author to experience success.
To find out how to publish your book, your way, and have it available
worldwide, visit us online at www.trafford.com*

Trafford rev. 5/22/2009

 www.trafford.com

North America & international
toll-free: 1 888 232 4444 (USA & Canada)
phone: 250 383 6864 ♦ fax: 250 383 6804 ♦ email: info@trafford.com

The United Kingdom & Europe
phone: +44 (0)1865 487 395 ♦ local rate: 0845 230 9601
facsimile: +44 (0)1865 481 507 ♦ email: info.uk@trafford.com

10 9 8 7 6 5 4 3 2 1

To:
Lauran, the "Iggy" of my group and my best friend.
Without you, this would all be just an idea in one of my dusty notebooks.

Prologue

Mariya swallowed and ran faster, pushing her muscles beyond their breaking point. She had been running for what seemed like hours now, and she felt as if she were about to collapse. Her stamina was higher than that of a human, but she knew she could not go on like this forever.

She glanced over her shoulder to see that the people following her had brought along bloodhounds. Mariya cursed to herself and pushed her already strained muscles even further. She winced as the soft fabric of her shoes caught on a vine and thorns embedded themselves in her soft flesh. She could feel the flow of the small stream of blood tracing the folds and lines in her skin, much like a river would to a canyon. The wails of the bloodhounds grew louder, filling the forest behind her with their call. Mariya's stomach ached when the vibrations from footsteps grew more rapid.

Closer.

Louder.

That damn vine, Mariya thought to herself, *It gave them my scent. Dammit . . . Dammit . . .*

One may wonder what Mariya was running from with so much integrity and passion. The answer is simple: Someone knew, someone found out. They found out what Mariya really is, and she hated herself for making such a stupid mistake. She had turned her attention for just a second, and someone caught her committing a taboo among humans: Drinking the blood of one of their kin.

She wanted to scream, but before any sound could leave her throat, her foot caught on a root. She let out a surprised squeak when her foot caught on and didn't come loose. Mariya stopped and freed her foot, but her dress caught on a briar bush near by.

Why can't anything go my way? Mariya asked herself, hastily and carefully coaxing the thorns from the tatty piece of fabric. She gave up and gave it a hard yank, falling over from the excess force of her pull. She caught herself on her hands, twisting her wrist and scratching her palms badly. She rubbed her head with her good hand, her mind racing through the possible outcomes of the situation. There was the crashing of feet through the underbrush, and Mariya looked up to the sight of boots, coupled by the faces of angry townspeople. She cursed to herself when a dog stepped forward and yelped at Mariya excitedly, its teeth bared. The men in the group chuckled amongst themselves, ugly grins distorting their faces.

This may be a stretch, Mariya thought to herself, *But dogs are related to wolves . . . and if the stories are true . . . vampires are related to wolves.* She took a deep breath and reached out to the dog with her mind, *Shh, peace cousin.* The dog stopped barking and locked gazes with Mariya as if it were entranced. Mariya started to feel a glimmer of hope but she continued carefully, *I'm on your side.*

The dog sat down and panted happily, its tail wagging rapidly. Mariya inwardly grinned, *Thank the gods for the myth being true.* The men all looked at one another, as hushed whispers of awe fell over the group.

The lead man stepped forward, "What's yer name, gal?"

Mariya blinked, "Excuse me?"

A lackey stepped forward and poked Mariya in her already sore calves with the hot barrel of a shotgun, "Tell 'im yer name!"

Mariya only rubbed the slight burn and bit her lip to prevent herself from saying anything on accident. "Yer young gal, you better tell 'im or else."

3

"Or else what?" Mariya demanded, her voice bold although she was shaking.

The lead man righted a shotgun he had been carrying under his arm. Mariya scowled, vampires were tough but guns could kill them. And they did not have to be any kind of special bullets. Holy water and crosses did nothing, and crucifixes only burned the skin slightly. The only thing from myth that could truly kill a vampire was a stake through the heart, but Mariya knew that in technicality it would kill *any* living thing. Sunlight did burn, but only after many hours of exposure would a vampire die. Even then, it would only kill a full vampire.

The man aimed the gun at point blank for Mariya, "Ir else yer dead."

She swallowed harshly and weakly whispered, "Mariya Gallion, a half-vampire."

Mariya surprised herself. Despite the hopelessness of the situation, her eyes gleamed brightly out of pride for her kind. Even staring down the barrel of a shotgun, she refused to be afraid. Acting on the false bravado, Mariya straightened herself up to look at the group of men that surrounded her. Every face in the group had turned white. A whisper fell over the group, and many took a couple steps back from her. The man with the shotgun looked shaken but still managed to snake his finger around the trigger and was just about to pull it when a young girl's voice burst through the wave of fear.

"Don't hurt her!" She pushed her way through the small crowd and stood in front of Mariya, her arms outstretched by her sides.

The man put his gun down, much to Mariya's relief. "Honey, I know you loves all livin' things, but she's one of them devils."

The girl turned to look at Mariya, beautiful blue eyes sparkling with the promise of life. "You're not a devil, are you?" She asked innocently, her eyes pleading with Mariya.

Mariya shook her head sadly, closing her eyes. "No, vampires aren't evil," her voice was thick with years of sorrow and shame.

"See, daddy?" The girl turned back to the man with the shotgun, "She's not evul, pweeze don't hurt her."

"Baby, I know you love all things, but she was drinkin' the blood of a man. . ."

Mariya stood up suddenly, "Such is our nature! Vampires don't persecute humans for what they are, do they?"

One of the other men spoke up, "We don't drink the life out of someone!"

"I, or any sane vampire for that matter, don't take the life of our victims," Mariya sighed, and as she continued her voice was even, yet at the same time, dripped acid. She glared at the group, eyeing up every member carefully, "I leave them with breath, their hearts still beating. It's wrong to take life, to destroy what's precious."

"How old are you gal?" The lead man asked, readying his gun.

"Eighty-eight." Mariya knew they wouldn't believe her though, because of the way vampires aged. She was blooded, or became a vampire, at two but eighty-six years had gone by and she only physically aged seventeen years. This was because full vampires age one year for every ten that go by, and half-vampires age half that. So, in other words, Mariya looked like she was about nineteen.

"Yeh right," The man laughed, "Tell us yer real age."

"Truly, I'm eighty-eight! I was born in November of nineteen-sixteen!" She pleaded with them, her eyes flashing a forest green.

"Daddy! She's not lying!" The girl pouted, "She's tellin' the twuth!"

"Fine," The man looked at Mariya, "You git one chance t'prove you ain't one of them devils. Otherwise," his voice trailed off in a menacing tone, glaring at her.

Mariya shivered just thinking about it. The man gave her one more angry glare, then the group cleared out. The girl smiled gratefully and looked at Mariya, "I'm Ivy."

Mariya nodded and kneeled. "Mariya Gallion," she

said and offered her hand for a shake.

Ivy hugged her instead. Mariya laughed and smoothed down her hair, and after a few moments Ivy let go and smiled. Mariya stood up and straightened out her skirt, just as the dog yelped happily and jumped in a circle around the two, eager to play.

Ivy smiled at Mariya, "That's Scout's way of saying he likes you."

1. In An Ordinary World

Mariya bolted upright, a cold sweat running over her. As usual when she woke up, her breath was uneven and heavy as her eyes anxiously scanned the room. Relieved, she let out a silent sigh and wiped the sleeve of her nightgown across her brow. Her breathing slowly faded back to its familiar rhythm and she was about to look up, when the door to her room opened slightly with a creak. Mariya immediately tensed, her heartbeat climbing already, but calmed down when a little girl ran in.

"Sissy!" The blonde girl cried and climbed onto Mariya's bed. Carefully, she settled into her lap, smiling when she draped one of the blankets over the girl's thin shoulders.

Mariya sighed and hugged the girl, "What's wrong sweetie?" She asked Ivy, a loving tone in her voice.

Ivy was barely ten, and already a beauty. Her golden blonde hair was almost always done up in a French braid. The braid was usually tied off with a satin ribbon, and the color varied depending on what she was wearing. Her blue eyes looked up at Mariya through a few strands of wispy hair.

"You were talking about that man is you sleep again, Sissy. Are you okay?" Ivy asked innocently.

Esiviel... She always called to him, her other half.

Mariya nodded. "Now, go help Papa make breakfast. I'll be out in a few minutes."

Ivy nodded eagerly and ran out of the room, rustling the carpet up on her way out. Mariya smiled and swung her long legs over the side of the bed. With a proud grin, she stretched and gave a twirl after standing up. Her nightgown flared out around her, then settled back down as she stopped. With a satisfied smile, Mariya went to her dresser. Tilting her head in thought, she turned this way and that, trying to get a good look at herself in the large mirror.

Mariya's skin was fair, almost ivory colored, like most of her lineage. Her eyes were a dark hazel, but would change forest green when she was startled or scared. Her

10

eyes looked back at herself through a few strands of dark hair that had escaped the larger lock of hair she called bangs. Beautiful raven black hair fell to her waist, where the ends started to wave.

I hate being like this, Mariya thought to herself before twirling again. She grimaced and closed the door to her room. She changed out of her silky nightgown into the velvet dress she had grown accustomed to wearing. It was made by Ivy's mother before she died, a present for one of her numerous birthdays. It was laced up the back like a corset, then tied loosely with a ribbon. It went to Mariya's ankles, the skirt made of a light and feathery fabric. Ivy's mother said it was to help her look more mysterious, and Mariya didn't mind the modest embellishment. All of it was a welcome change from the lavish conditions she had grown up in.

She untucked her dark hair from the collar with a contented sigh and tied it up in a black satin ribbon. Looking at herself in the mirror one more time, Mariya smiled in her mysterious way and went to the kitchen.

As soon as Mariya walked into the kitchen, she could tell something was wrong. Scout, the family dog, didn't run to meet her like usual. Deryk, Ivy's father, sat quietly at the table, reading the daily paper. His hand covered the article, but Mariya could see the headlines:

'Mysterious Murders: Could it be the work of

vampires?'

Mariya's eyes went wide in fear; she knew what that meant. This house would no longer be a haven because of her presence. Regardless, Deryk regarded her calmly.

"Mariya, could you make breakfast for Ivy today?" She could tell he was trying to keep his voice even and measured.

Mariya nodded and looked at Ivy, kneeling to her level. "Should I make my special pancakes?" She asked sweetly, even though her eyes showed otherwise. Ivy smiled broadly and nodded eagerly. With a smile, Mariya ruffled Ivy's hair then went about making her 'special pancakes.'

They really weren't out of the ordinary. Mariya just used more egg and less milk, making them thicker. Sometimes, she would add brown sugar to give them a 'melt-in-your-mouth' taste. Twenty minutes later, Ivy was sitting at the dining room table in the sun room. The sun shone through the frosted glass, giving the plants in the room a wet look. The rose bushes outside had grown up the side of the room, covering it with a red and green canopy. Mariya placed a plate full of pancakes in front of Ivy, covered in homemade blackberry syrup from her grandmother Rosa's recipe. Ivy's eyes lit up.

"Thank you, Sissy!"

"Say grace," Mariya reminded Ivy gently and poured her a glass of juice.

Ivy nodded and folded her hands together, bowing her head. "Thank you God for all the wonderful things you give me. Please bless Papa and Sissy, and thank you for the food. In your name I pray. Amen."

Mariya sat in the kitchen with Deryk, and neither said a word. The air around them was tense, thick. Mariya had trouble deciding whether it was from the heat of the sun, or the awkward silence that had enveloped the two of them. Finally, Deryk spoke up when she went to get a cup of coffee.

"Mariya," He started calmly, although his voice was tense, "Have you fed this month?"

Mariya dropped two sugar cubes in her cup and stirred, "Not yet, no. Why?"

"There are reports of corpses turning up in the sewers, and other places in town, drained of blood," Deryk looked at Mariya carefully, trying to measure her reaction. It was as if he thought he could lift the truth, or at least what he wanted, from her mind just by staring.

Mariya gagged, choking on her coffee. She coughed wildly out of surprise. "And you think I would do that?!" She retorted hotly once she regained herself, her temper flaring. "You know I respect all life!"

"I know," Deryk replied calmly while folding up the newspaper, "But who else would do it?"

Mariya sighed and went over to the table, not even

having to try. She just appeared, almost teleporting across the kitchen. Deryk blinked and she was standing next to him, looking at him with sagacious patience in her hazel eyes. "Vampires are fairly common, Deryk. It could just be a rogue seeking out attention, or a fledgling that hasn't learned its place yet."

The room fell silent again after Mariya's explanation, until Ivy ran in from the dining room. Without saying a word, Mariya turned and helped Ivy with the dishes. After the dishes were done, it was decided that the two would go shopping in town to look at the merchants that were visiting for the season.

Once Ivy was properly dressed, Mariya shooed her out of the house, aware of the fact that Deryk was watching her with more curiosity than necessary. She paused in the doorway to look at him and muttered:

"Don't worry. I'll protect you both, no matter what. This is *my* territory."

2. Let Me Bleed You A Song

The stares of the townsfolk were piercing, stabbing, maybe even strong enough to murder. Even though they stopped when Mariya looked, hushed whispers would spread. *They think I'm the killer,* Mariya thought as Ivy stepped closer to her for comfort and clutched her hand tightly, *They think I'm the monster behind all of this.*

It had been two weeks since the mysterious murders had started, and now the rumors of Mariya had spread like wildfire across the small Italian city. Now, Mariya couldn't even go into a bakery without a stare or a whisper being dispersed through the room. Sadly, she had been treated like any other person before this. Now, she seemed to be the scum of the Earth.

Mariya readjusted her parasol again and let Ivy pull her over to a small jewelry stand. Her eyes sparkled as she looked at the treasures; and then held up a tiny, silver cross for Mariya to see.

"Please, Sissy?" Ivy asked, her eyes pleading with Mariya.

Mariya took the cross from Ivy and held it flat in her palm. The shop-keep laughed half-heartedly, "Shouldn't you be burning up?"

Mariya laughed bitterly and held the cross up to the sun to see all of its faults. "You believe that old myth?" She asked with mild curiosity, looking at the man out of the corner of her eyes.

"Why wouldn't I?" The shopkeeper looked taken aback.

Mariya smiled and handed the cross the back to Ivy, as well as enough money to pay for it. "You can't believe everything you hear. Why would a cross hurt me?" She looked the store owner in the eyes, daring him to give her the answer that she knew was coming. She reached out to his mind with hers, and saw he was struggling to get an answer. That was until the memories of Sunday school came back.

Therefor I said unto the children of Israel, No soul of you shall eat blood, neither shall any stranger that sojourenth among you eat blood. . .

"Because you're-!"

16

Mariya cut him off, "Because I'm evil?" With a knowing smile, she carefully laid down her parasol and helped Ivy put the cross on her silver necklace chain.

"Y-yes. . ."

"So I'm a hunter," Mariya stood up straightened out her skirt. "I rely on humans for life like you do your livestock and crops. It's no different, am I wrong?" She looked at the man as he babbled incoherently, trying to come up with a valid response. With a mocking curtsey, she picked up her parasol and took Ivy's hand. "Good day, sir."

The people watched Mariya closely, almost daring her to do something unjust. She merely paid them no mind, but Ivy wasn't as seasoned to such treatment. She stepped as close as she could to Mariya, gripping her hand tightly.

"Sissy," Ivy spoke up, her voice shaking.

Mariya didn't hear her. She was too lost in her own thoughts, in remembrance. Something like this had passed before, and now it was coming again. It was the cycle of death, all because of her father. Every town she left was left behind in ruins, chaos. The roads were stained red with the blood of his victims and rotting corpses would line the streets. And now he had followed Mariya to this peaceful village in Italy. He always followed her like a shadow she couldn't get rid of, no matter how long she hid in the dark. He was her grim reaper, casting a shadow on the land and claiming the lives of it as his own.

It was complicated game of cat and mouse. Neither knew whether they were the one doing the chasing or the one being chased. Like the ouroboros, the predator could be the same as the prey. Yin and Yang.

Life and death.

To make matters worse, Mariya had grown close to a human. She hated herself for it part of the time; she had given herself a weakness. The other part of the time she was perfectly happy, playing the role of Ivy's mother.

"Sissy?" Ivy repeated louder, tugging on Mariya's skirt nervously.

Mariya blinked, suddenly pulled to attention. "Huh?" She looked at Ivy with a look of bewilderment, "What's wrong sweetie?"

"They're watching us..." She looked around nervously, her blue eyes filled with unease.

Mariya looked straight forward, her eyes filled with pride, "Never mind them. Think tall, walk proudly. "

"But Sissy..."

"Don't be afraid, Ivy," she gave Ivy's hand a reassuring squeeze, "I'm here for you." In a quite voice, she promised, "And I will never let *anything* happen to you."

Ivy looked up at Mariya in surprise. Mariya was known to be loving, but was not one known for coming out like that. She was usually so shrouded in mystery, but for once, she was open. She was like a sister, almost mother, to Ivy and she took the role seriously. If nothing else, she wanted Ivy to grow up to be a well-respected young woman, as though to protect her from the ridicule Mariya had faced in *her* lifetime. Yet, Ivy was young and innocent, and sometimes things like that just went over her head.

It was midday when the two returned to the ivy covered brick house in the back of the foothills. It was set on a hill that overlooked the landscape for miles, and the porch was the best place in the entire town place to watch the sunset. It was made entirely of old-fashioned red brick and had frosted glass windows. All of the flowerbeds in the front were full of rose bushes, the pride of the town.

They were a special type that only bloomed at full moon, and when they did, it was a sight unlike any other. They were pure white, save for the veins of red that flowed through the outer petals. It was because of these 'veins' the rose earned its name: The blood rose. When one bloomed, Mariya would carefully pick it and put it a glass of water for Ivy, where it would last for weeks.

Pausing as she reached for the door, Mariya sighed. She knew this day would come eventually, but she never thought so soon. How was she going to tell her mate? Or, better yet, young Ivy? Surely she wouldn't understand the dangers and only think Mariya was being mean. Gathering up some confidence, Mariya turned and knelt to Ivy's level.

"Sweetie, you know how I sometimes I bring you out at night with me?" Mariya asked in a level tone of voice, not showing the fear in her.

"Yeah!" Ivy's face lit up.

"I can't bring you with me anymore," Mariya said flatly, striving for authoritative.

"Why not?" Ivy demanded, her eyes pleading.

Mariya ignored it, knowing it was for the best. "I don't want you getting hurt, sweetie. . ." she reached out to smooth down Ivy's unruly hair.

Ivy pulled away, "Why? What'll happen if I come?" She crossed her arms against her chest and got her usual stubborn look.

With a sigh, Mariya let her hand fall to her side again, "With everything that has been happening, it would be safer for you."

"But Sissy!" Ivy protested.

Mariya sighed and tried to stay steady. This had to be done, especially with the murder victims all being the in same age range as Ivy. Even then, it was hard not to get soft when talking to Ivy, so much so that now Mariya's friends joked she did not have a backbone, that living with humans had made her lose her vampiric edge. They all knew Mariya still had a vampire's heart, though. She loved to listen to the lifetime of stories taught by the moonlight and dance in the star lit nights to the rhythm of the dark. She was very in tune with spirit of the night, but that was not enough. Unlike Mariya, her father did not fear the vampire in him. He welcomed it, and had learned to control his abilities to their maximum potential. Also unlike his daughter, Mariya's father, Devon, was of full blood.

This was only accomplished when an individual dies as a half-vampire, usually along the lines of bleeding to death or drowning. It was uncommon; so many vampires were pure blood from their blooding, or birth, to prevent the horrible after affects of dying. For Mariya, it did not matter. She wanted the freedom of a human, but even then it was not her choice to join the ranks of the undead. She was born part vampire, but her blood took hold of her heart when she was two, sending her into the jurisdiction of the moon.

"No, and that's the final word," Mariya said, her voice sure. She got up and took Ivy's hand, who looked at the ground sadly. *Sorry Ivy,* Mariya thought to herself as she led Ivy inside, *But I can't let you be my fault.*

3. In The Shadow Of The Lies

It seemed like any other time that Mariya had awoken at night. Moonlight gently streamed through the dark draperies and bathed the entire room in its silver glow. The shadows were long and drawn out, nothing like they would be in the daytime. Mariya welcomed this time of day, the time when all things seemed romantic and mysterious. It was when all edges were soft, and even the sternest person looked calm. Above that, it made her blood sing, her muscles and flesh ache to run. She would always want to listen, and never look back.

Mariya blinked and looked out at the glitter that the gods had spilt. They hung in a purple tinted background, but shined so brightly against the dark sky of the night. They invited her to come out and play, to visit the darkness just once. Just to remember what her life was tied to. Stifling a yawn, Mariya sat up and stretched. It was completely silent, nearing midnight. It was also the perfect time for this.

She was meeting with Esiviel today, and she couldn't be happier. He was older than her, much older. He was very wise in the ways of their kin, and he had taught Mariya almost everything she knew.

With a smile, Mariya tied her hair back in its usual black satin ribbon. Her hazel eyes shined brightly out of hope, but were shadowed deep down with despair. Her father's evident appearance had made her restless. But she hoped this meeting would be a welcome reprieve from the recent chaos of her life.

As promised, Esiviel was waiting for her on the edge of town. He was always a sight to be seen, and tonight was no exception. His silver eyes stared back at the world from beneath his dark bangs. Like usual, he was dressed in his favorite white trench coat, the belt undone and hanging loosely by his sides. Under his trench coat he wore a pair of ratty blue jeans and a navy colored tank top that clung to his lean figure. He was already tall, but his lean build made him seem even taller.

"Hello, Mariya," He spoke in a calm voice. It was always like that, gentle, mild, even. The only time it had escaped those boundaries was the last time the two ran into Mariya's father. A horrible fight had ensued, and left

Esiviel with a scar that stretched across his chest.

Mariya smiled when he stepped out of the shadows of the tree he had been standing under. *Gawd he's gorgeous*, she thought to herself, noticing the way the moon lit his skin perfectly and made him look like one of the living. But her smile was short lived and she looked at the ground guiltily, her bangs hiding her face. Silent tears rolled down her cheeks, but she refused to accept that they were there.

"Mariya?" Esiviel walked over and tenderly put a hand on her shoulder, "What's wrong?"

"It's nothing, Esiviel," Mariya looked away.

He sighed, she was always like this. Mariya was a wonderful listener and such a patient person, but when *she* was the one that needed to talk, she shied away from it. And she would stay that way, even when she couldn't hold her problems and fears in, she tried to until it all boiled over and she broke. Only then, it was the complete feeling of helplessness that made her admit.

"Mariya," Esiviel's voice grew impatient, maybe even admonitory. He put his hand under her chin and tilted her head up so she had to look up at him. Her hazel eyes met his, fogged over slightly and tearing at the corners. "What's wrong?" He asked again, his voice firm.

"I think my father's in town," Mariya said plainly, her voice flat.

Any color left in Esiviel's skin was immediately

25

flushed out. His eyes flashed a dark brown, showing the fault in his blood. It was like when Mariya's flashed green, just a fight-or-flight reaction. He quickly turned away, shading his eyes with his hand as if the sun was beating down on him. He feared Mariya's father more than anyone, anything. The mere mention of his name made the scar on his chest burn. "Are you sure?" He asked, his voice, and body, shaking.

Mariya nervously clasped her necklace in both hands. She nodded mutely even though both knew there wasn't the need for a confirmation.

Mariya was right.

Hell was back.

Mariya immediately broke down into tears, but only quiet sobs. Her entire body shook from the effort of holding in the tears, and a rough cotton ball soon formed in her throat. She swallowed many times, willing herself to calm down. Even when she closed her eyes, that haunting memory came back:

It was a chilling night, late December. It was when Mariya was three in human years, just learning to walk and understand the life around her. She awakened from a nightmare in the middle of the night, and ventured out into the cold of the hallway to go to her mother's room. The huge mansion was lavishly decorated, usually so welcoming. Yet, the darkness made the house seem like a Halloween attraction, so Mariya picked up her pace.

The door to her mother's room was cracked, candlelight flittering out into the hallway. Curiously, Mariya peeked in through the crack, but quickly withdrew. Her mother, beautiful and frail looking, was sprawled out on the floor, surrounded by a pool of blood. She tried to scream, but a gentle hand was placed over her mouth and she was whisked away from that house of death by her guardian, Zethin. She could still remember the ice cold rain picking up as she clutched his hand tightly and ran into the night in a helpless flight.

And now he's here.

For me.

And death follows until he finds me.

She looked at the ground, her chin touching her chest. Mariya didn't want Esiviel to see her like this, she was supposed to be the strong one. Yet, here she was, haunted by a memory nearly a century old, the threat of it happening again hanging in front of her face.

It had been like this for as long as Mariya could remember, ever since that desperate night of running, she had always been on the move. She couldn't now, though, she swore to protect Ivy, even if it meant the death of her kin. She had sworn a blood oath. Yet, even with the threat of her own life in danger, Mariya never ran for herself, it was Esiviel. She was royalty, he her guardian. The quickest way to kill the queen was to kill the one that was sworn to her by oath, her lover. He would never tell why he took that oath, and Mariya never questioned it. The two were always together, though, inseparable.

Swiftly, Mariya found herself in Esivel's arms. He held her close, tightly, as if he could protect her from the world. It was the sweetest thing, but she got no sense of heat from him. This was because Esiviel was of pure blood.

Dead to the world.

His heart still beat, but slowly. Even slower, his blood crawled through his veins. He didn't need to breathe either, and he only did so out of a need to talk. The sun no longer lit his skin, but his eyes still sparkled with life. Despite all of that, though, he felt alive.

"Shh," he whispered, smoothing down her hair, "No tears, my love."

"But I don't want to…" Mariya started to whimper, her voice muffled because she buried her face in his shoulder.

"We're not going to run again," Esiviel promised and held her tighter. "Not this time."

Mariya returned home around dawn, just as the sun was peaking over the horizon. She felt calmed in a way, but that serenity was short lived when skinny arms were wrapped around her waist as soon as she stepped foot on the lawn.

"Sissy!"

Mariya smiled with a sigh and knelt to Ivy's level. "What's wrong sweetie?" She asked gently, smoothing down Ivy's rumpled hair.

Ivy looked at the ground, nervously twisting the hem of her shirt between her fingers, "Daddy wants to talk to you." She looked at Mariya with pleading eyes, "He sounded really upset."

Maryia sighed and put a hand on Ivy's shoulder, "I'm sure it's nothing." She assured her, ignoring the inner panic, "We'll go talk to him right now, okay?" She smiled and got up, straightening out her skirt.

"But Sissy!!!" Ivy impatiently stamped her foot, "He's *really* upset! He kept somethin' about you being one them devuls!"

Mariya froze midstep, and her breath caught in her throat. *Sweet moon,* she thought, *Does he still blame me for all of this?* Deryk was the mayor of the town, and it was understandable that he wanted to find the murderer, but blaming an innocent young woman? Vampire or not, it enraged Mariya. It also reminded her of how fickle human nature could be, how afraid of the unknown they were. Deryk didn't know much about the true nature of most vampires, so he immediately placed it on the closest one.

Mariya.

He had blamed her for things before, as if he *wanted* to get rid of her. And truth be told, she was guilty of some minor crimes, but not as high as the ones that Deryk blamed her for. Murder? Mariya's conscience would have killed her before she got away with it. He *was* eager to get rid of her and her mate, human nature at its best.

Fear.

Pure and simple.

Mariya drew in a shuddering breath and tried to relax. She smiled at Ivy, trying for motherly, "How about you go work in the rose garden for a few minutes? I'll be there soon."

Ivy smiled brightly, problem forgotten, and nodded eagerly, "Okay!"

Watching her run off, Mariya called after Ivy, "Remember to wear gloves!"

With a loving smile, but a nervous sigh, Mariya went inside. Her insides were all bound into knots, making her feel sick. Her breaths were uneven, but after some struggling, she got that under control. The walk down the hall to the living room was almost like death row. She had a feeling of impending danger, although she knew not much could hurt her that badly. Before leaving the parlor, she calmed down, looking at herself in the sun-shaped mirror that hung on the wall. *It'll be okay*, she thought as if to encourage herself. *He needs you to take care of Ivy.*

She found Deryk in the living room, relaxing in his favorite armchair and reading over the Sunday paper. "Yes, sir?" She gave a weak curtsy, almost feeling like a maid instead of a stand-in nanny.

He nodded in acknowledgment, "Where were you last night?"

"Why should I tell you?!" Mariya demanded, "I can take care of myself without some nosey cop-wannabe having to give me the third degree in my own haven!"

"Just answer the question!"

Mariya sighed and glared at him, her gaze dripping icicles, "With my mate, Esiviel Colombain. No, we *did not* feed last night. I just..."

"What about..."

"No!" Mariya screamed, her temper flaring, "Esiviel and I did nothing!" She quickly turned on her heels and *ran* outside, acting more like a young runaway princess instead of the soon-to-be queen she was. Ignoring Ivy's calls, she darted down the dirt path.

After nearly thirty minutes, she collapsed under an oak tree. Her chest rose and fell rapidly, her lungs burning for oxygen. Mariya winced; her throat felt as if someone had ran their nails down it. She coughed weakly and rolled on her side. It hurt everywhere, and she tried to loosen up, but she couldn't.

Her muscles screamed to run.
Her lungs ached for air.
Her eyes stung from the wind.
She could barely keep her eyes open.

I can stay here, she thought as her eyes fluttered shut, *Just until. . .I. . .rest ...*

31

4. The Dark Within the Soul

Summer slowly crawled by and gradually faded into autumn and even the earth began to feel it. The air cooled, and the once golden waves of grain turned to a light brown as the plants wilted and sagged. The trees showed off their annual display of fireworks, and the world was filled with activity. Many of the traders and craftsmen left to find more favorable climates, promising to return when the sun returned to the grey sky. Town was quiet, but somehow Mariya didn't feel the drag of the humans. She was giddy, anxious, as if waiting in anticipation for a celebration. Her blood boiled for activity, but she willed it down with the thought of snow soon to fall.

Even Esiviel felt the change in not just the earth, but the energy and spirit of the land was different, twisted, and unsettling. His return from his annual journeys brought excitement, but Mariya was too exhausted to give him a proper return.

"You've been neglecting your feedings again, haven't you?" He looked her over, sympathy in his words.

"It's hard…with the murders…"

"I know," he smiled, ruffling her hair and kissing her gently.

The murders had eased up for awhile, but things were just as tense for Mariya. She couldn't even walk through town without a whisper spreading over the crowd. Sometimes people would stop her to ask half-heartedly about the murders, but cower out of childish fear of the unknown. Some would even joke of what she did with the bodies after she drained them of their blood. She would only turn the other cheek and ignore them.

Now, she almost always wore a gothic-style cross on a crimson ribbon around her neck as a choker. It was under the order of Deryk in an attempt to show the villagers that Mariya wasn't evil. Nevertheless, whispers still spread and mothers, tired with the day's work, would hurry their children inside and close the shutters behind them.

Just as the town slowly turned to a ghost town because of Mariya's presence, a shadow grew over her loving heart. She began to grow solitary, and soon didn't even bother to sneak out to meet with Esiviel. She went from being a social butterfly, to the spider in the corner.

Feared by all, loved by few.

One particular day, she sat by the window of her room and looked at her reflection in the antique glass. Her eyes had lost their glow long ago, and were now a dull hazel; much like a nut that had been buried for several months, then dug back up. Her skin was extremely pale from the absence of the sun, for she didn't leave the house unless absolutely necessary. With a sigh, she looked away from her pitiful reflection and slipped on her shoes. Mariya had lost hope, and as far as she was concerned, she was never going to regain it.

She opened the front door with a creak, hesitating for a minute. Her hand barely gripped the handle, and she had no presence. She was just there. Right before she stepped out, Deryk called her.

"Mariya!" She weakly looked up at him, "Here."

He handed her a parchment envelope with her name written on the front in a flourishing script. For a moment, Mariya stared blankly at the package, then shrugged and put it on the counter in the kitchen.

"I'll open it later," she muttered weakly.

"But…"

Mariya shook her head regretfully, "No. I *have* to feed."

Feed.

That word shook Deryk to the core of his existence. It still made no sense to him how something as gentle as Mariya would commit such a heinous act. It sent chills down his spine to imagine her sinking her fangs into someone's skin, and drinking their very life force without second thought. It made her seem like an angel of death, and in a way, she was.

Mariya went to a local club, a quick and easy way to get a free meal. The night was inviting though, the sights and sounds all trying to pull her in. The calls of the bugs echoed through the air, each playing their own part to a perfectly orchestrated musical spectacular. It all excited Mariya, trying to resist the urge to dance to the calls of the darkness under the moonlight.

Regretfully, she ignored the pull of her instincts and stepped into the bright lights and loud sounds of the club. Like usual, she ordered brandy on the rocks then went to find her newest prey.

Mariya settled herself in the corner of the one-room brick building and carefully watched every person, calculating her chances. She sipped at her drink slowly, disappointed at the lack of interesting entrees on the menu. She sighed and almost gave up when she spotted something interesting.

He was tall and skinny. He was something that humans would dream about, bright eyes and hair cut so

36

that it covered one eye. Mariya smiled; if he was drunk, this would be easy. Too easy. She effortlessly picked her way across the crowd and seated herself on a stool next to the boy.

He was laughing at a joke from one of his friends, and ordered some expensive import beer. Mariya sighed dejectedly and gracefully brushed her hair over shoulder with a flick of her wrist. She rolled her shoulders slightly, hoping it helped that her dress strap slipped slightly. Just like she planned, the boy noticed.

"Hey," he said with a slight drunken tone, eyeing her up. Mariya looked at him innocently, totally irresistible. "Can I buy you a drink?"

"Who?" She tried to make herself seem clueless, "Me?" She grinned and let her eyes close to small slits in mock desire, "Could we just skip the formalities?" *Careful Mariya*, she coached herself. *Don't lose yourself.*

The boy blinked, dumbfounded. "Um....sure."

With a teasing wink, she slipped off the stool and made her way across the room. Mariya led him to one of the darkest corners of the room, and made sure to swing her hips in a way that would keep the boy looking at her. She smiled at him, and he carefully slipped his arms around her waist and kissed her passionately. Mariya drew in a deep breath, willing down the swift pang that went straight through her. *It's not for him*, Mariya reminded herself. He kissed her neck, and she grinned, the fatal mistake all humans made.

"Hush, little one," she whispered, slipping her arms around him. "Shh."

She kissed his neck gently and she felt he was in her grasp; she gave him the sweet silver kiss.

Sweet warmth.
Indescribable heat.

The boy shuddered as her fangs slid into his skin, then settled down with a happy sigh. He almost cooed when she began to drink, and it was a struggle for Mariya not to grin. Humans were so susceptible, this all was almost too easy. Then again, she did have rely on a trait that vampires had developed. There was a sort of sedative in their spit that calmed the victim down and prevented them from running away. Yet, in a way, it didn't make sense to Mariya. She wondered why it have even come about, seeing as it was already nearly impossible to get away from a feeding vampire.

Regardless, she still had to be careful with which humans she chose. Mariya couldn't make a pact with one and keep feeding from them, it would be dangerous for the human. Many had figured this out in the past, when their "host" seemed to be unable to leave. This was because of the drug-like qualities of their spit. Like many powerful pain killers, it was addictive. After several times experiencing it, it varied depending on the person's ability to metabolize it, they began to acquire a psychological need for it. Sighing, Mariya pushed away the troubled thoughts and focused on the task at hand.

His life played before her eyes, showing everything he had been through. She ignored the images of baseball games with dad, washing dishes after making cookies with mom, or even his first time having sex. It all meant nothing to Mariya. She slowly felt herself slipping as well, and she tried to pull away.

She couldn't.

She didn't want to.

Mariya calmed down and took a deep breath, then pulled her fangs in. She pushed the boy away quickly, gasping out of fear. Mariya knew how close she had come to killing him, how badly her body wanted blood. She had felt his heartbeat slow and his breathing grow labored, right in her arms. She almost broke her oath and killed, it scared her so badly. She ran as fast as her legs would carry her, the boy's blood settling heavily in her stomach and on her gums.

Run, *that's the only thought that echoed through Mariya's mind.* Run, *save yourself. It was the same as any of Mariya's other nightmares. Running, screaming, getting hurt. She would get in trouble for something, then run until her legs couldn't carry her anymore. And beyond sometimes.*

Her muscles burned, and her lungs worked frantically to

get enough oxygen into her. Each breath became harder than the last, making her sides ache and beg her to stop. It felt like someone had stabbed her, but she insisted on running.

No matter what.

She desperately flung the door to her room open, the door hitting the wall behind it with a loud thud. Mariya's mind was racing, a million and a half thoughts flying through her brain at once. She took several deep breaths, and calmed down her pounding heart. She sat down on the thick blankets of her bed, sinking into the oblivion of the mattress. Mariya began to calm down, her mind straightening itself out. Then there was a loud creak in the corner, and Mariya snapped to attention. There was nothing, or no one, there.

Nothing.
Not a thing.

There was a gift box on her bureau, tied up by a crimson ribbon. With a confused blink, Mariya forced her aching form to investigate. It seemed like any other package from the outside when Mariya rolled it around in her hands. It was a completely seamless box, save for the crease from where the top opened. She suddenly froze when she felt a warm sensation running down her arm.

There was a crimson liquid flowing from a hole in the box. It streamed down Mariya's arm, where it pooled in the palm of her outstretched hand. She nearly dropped the package, but forced herself to stay calm. She curiously tasted the liquid, and gaged.

It was Esiviel's blood.

Mariya readjusted her grip on the package. Her insides were all looped into knots, making her sick. A bile rose in her throat, dreading what was in the package. Part of her screamed to put it down and run, but she couldn't bring herself to.

Curiosity killed the cat.

She cautiously opened the package and peered inside through the small crack she had made. Mariya immediately let out a scream and dropped the box, taking several frightened steps back. Inside was Esiviel, chopped into bits. Mariya covered her eyes with clasped hands, but it was no use, the image was burned into her eyes. The carpet glinted wetly and the smell of his blood quickly filled the small room like cheap cologne.

And satisfaction brought it back?

Mariya gaged, letting the small whimper in her throat take form. She shook her head in denial, just hoping it was a nightmare. As if the realization finally hit her, she fell to her knees and buried her face in her hands and wept.

For awhile she grieved, crying in that tomb of death. After some time, Mariya had no idea how long, a piece of parchment flittered to the floor. It was folded into its own envelope, with her name on it in a flourishing script. Mariya tentatively reached for the paper. After a moment of hesitation, Mariya's fingers clumsily fumbled with the flap. In a script similar to the one on the front, the inside read:

41

My Dearest Mariya,

How did you like your present? Life's not fair, is it? How would you like to know that there is much more to come? It is, after all, your fault he's dead. Your family will always suffer. Watch your back, darling, or you may be the next one in the box.

Mariya panted and moaned, tossing and turning. There was a strong tugging in her chest, although she was fast asleep. It couldn't be true, could it? A single tear ran down her cheek, and lay still for a moment before the fits began again.

"Esiviel!" She bolted upright, gasping.

Mariya looked around the room nervously, her heavy panting the loudest sound in the room. After regaining herself, she flung her bedcovers aside and swung her legs over the edge of the bed. Barely pausing to slip on her ballet flats or change, she darted out of the house into the night.

This couldn't, wouldn't, wait. Esiviel meant the world to Mariya, and she had to make sure he was okay. She checked all of his favorite places, but found no sign of him. Even his favorite outcropping overlooking the town was empty, except for a scrap of white fabric. Mariya knew it to be a shred of his trench coat, so at least he had put up a fight. Shakily, she picked up the white shard and ran a finger over the familiar, smooth material.

A lump of cotton formed in her throat, and she fought it back down. Her eyes hazed, and tears poured down her porcelain cheeks. She knew what it meant, and prayed for a miracle.

Her nightmare was real.

And if Esiviel wasn't dead, he soon would be. If he wasn't, he would wish he was. Death would be the only blessing in his now dark existence.

5. The Shadow Darkens

"Hey," came a gentle voice that swept through her sleep.

It was like autumn leaves slowly dancing and twisting to the ground in the light breeze. It was comfort after a chaotic day, sweet and patient. There was a soft hand on her shoulder, pulling her from her nightmares and back into reality.

Mariya blinked in the blinding afternoon light, struggling to focus on the person. It was a older boy, maybe in his late teens or early twenties. He had long blue-tinted hair tied back in a ponytail. He wore a collared white shirt with old fashioned blue jeans. Over that, he wore a long, black leather coat that had many belts on the shoulders that hung undone. The silver buckles sparkled brightly, much like the young man's eyes. He looked like the opposite of Esiviel, a more gothic version. Upon closer inspection, Mariya learned he also wore gloves that looked much like a bikers and a silver cross choker.

"Wha. . .?" Mariya mumbled lazily, sitting up.

"Are you okay?" The boy asked with genuine concern, sympathy lighting his harvest gold eyes.

Mariya went to rub her head, but froze when she saw the shred of fabric in her hand. She almost immediately choked up again, swallowing several times to get her tears under control. It was no good, though, to her dismay.

After several minutes, Mariya managed to turn her tears of ice into shudders. She blushed, embarrassed to be seen like this by a complete stranger. It was silent for the longest time in that darkened cavern, the hypnotic sound of dripping echoing to the front from far off into the darkness. Although Mariya's eyes were fixed on the rough floor of that shallow cave, she could feel the boy's eyes on her.

"What?!!" she snapped, annoyed the boy hadn't said anything yet.

"Why were you out here all alone?" the boy asked, "Especially out here on the edge of town, it's dangerous."

"Why should you care?" Mariya grumbled, annoyed at the boy's interest. "You don't even know me," She muttered to herself, more of an after thought. She sighed dejectedly, opening her mouth wide to get a deep breath. The boy's eyes flashed with interest, his eyes going wide. "What?!" Mariya snapped, looking at him oddly.

"Are your teeth always that sharp?"

"Well, duh," Mariya was surprised into saying, letting out a startled laugh. "I kinda *need* my fangs to live. Why?"

The boy shook his head in dismissal, "No reason."

Mariya eyed him warily, fear growing in her chest. Her heartbeat picked up and her breathing grew more rapid to pump more oxygen into her. He knew, he knew about her being a vampiress. Did he want to kill her? She couldn't be sure anymore, the murders had made her public image suffer. It seemed like everyone was either afraid of her or out for her blood.

Mariya eyes flashed a forest green in their normal fight or flight response, and stayed that way.

The color swirled like a gas against the black of her pupils and the white of her irises. It danced calmly, then the motion would grow hyperactive and swirl around hastily as if it responded to Mariya's thoughts. They were the reflection of her soul, her most intimate thoughts that not even the moon knew, being projected to the world. They seemed to have a life of their own, and the boy noticed.

"Don't be afraid," he coaxed, "I won't hurt you." He continued in a quieter, gentler tone of voice. "I've been

47

interested in the occult for awhile, and I just noticed your eyes and fangs. . ." He smiled at her, "It just adds up. But why are you wearing a cross? It doesn't suit someone like you."

Mariya sighed in defeat and took a moment to calm herself, her eyes returning to their usual color. "You're right," she whispered lowly, "I'm one of the cursed few destined for darkness." She put her hand over the silver cross around her neck, "And this is my way of showing the bumbling idiots of the town that I reside in that my kind is not evil."

"Oh," the boy looked taken aback, "It just doesn't seem like it would suit you."

Mariya laughed. She was intrigued by the boy's enthusiasm. It was refreshing to find a person among the living that actually seemed to understand her kind. Maybe, for once, she would play with her food. Mariya shook off the idea. She was in deep enough trouble as is, and she didn't need to be causing any more mischief. There wasn't a need to stir up the humans more than absolutely necessary.

"Well," Mariya sighed and stood up, "Thank you for your concern, but I must be going." She turned to leave and enjoyed it as the rays of the sun warmly lit her skin.

"Wait!" the boy stood up as well, "What's your name?"

Mariya wistfully looked at sky, "Mariya Gallion."

"Mariya. . ." the boy repeated, letting it settle in his mind, "Are you Russian?"

"No, pure blood Italian. But that's beside the point. Yours?"

"Kristopher," the boy stated proudly.

Mariya smiled, *He's so much like Esiviel. He's a prideful idiot who tries to act calm, but is really a wreck inside. Except Esiviel is a better actor than this guy.* "Thank you, Kristopher," she bowed her head in respect.

Kristopher's face lit with a blush, and he quickly changed the subject. "What's the fabric?"

"Nothing," Mariya said with a warning tone in her voice, her eyes cold.

"Really," Kristopher prodded as if her annoyance meant nothing to him, "What is it?"

Mariya hesitated for a moment, then sighed. "It's a piece of fabric torn from my lover's coat. He's been taken, and if you excuse me, I must set about finding him." Mariya nodded and took a step into the bright afternoon light.

"Wait!" Kristopher called after her, making her pause, "I can help."

"How?" Mariya asked, not turning to look at him.

Kristopher smiled brightly, "I have my ways."

Mariya returned home, her mind racing. Just who was this Kristopher and why did he just offer her help like that? *It could be a trap,* Mariya thought, *Or, he could be one of those people that just wants to help.* She laughed bitterly to herself, *Yeah right, like that'll happen this late in the game.*

Mariya slipped off her sun dress and looked at her thin frame in the mirror. It had been several days since Esiviel was taken, and her health began to show it. She didn't eat much anymore, so her weight lost was evident. The ticking of the clock on the wall didn't make it any better. Each passing second made her more and more anxious. Each tick seemed to pound in her head, reminding her of her one fatal mistake.

Birth.

Existence.

She closed her eyes and tried to fight off the pitiful tears that welled to the surface. She leaned against a wall slightly, hating every minute of this. Mariya hated feeling so weak, so helpless. This vulnerability consumed her, and she loathed herself for it. Memories of the two of them flashed in her mind.

Esiviel brushing the hair out of her face then kissing her with a twinkle in his eye.

Her laughing at some joke he had made.

Esiviel holding her close when she was afraid, protecting her.

The night they met.

Mariya was a mess back then, a total wreck. The night was always vivid in her mind as if it had been burned into her eyes:

50

"Haha! Sissie!" The young men all laughed and chanted. They kicked and punched her, making the bruises she already had grow larger. She fell to her knees whimpering, clutching her hands against her chest. Mariya always took this beating without complaint. If she did say anything, they would tell everyone her true nature.

She looked up through tear-streaked eyes and saw a man watching from the shadows of the tree line. He watched Mariya intently, regarding the others with a glowing hatred in his silver eyes. The entire world seemed quiet when Mariya locked gazes with him.

For a moment, she lost herself in his eyes, and his never left hers. It was like he was talking to her, soothing her pain and telling her that he understood. Right before she fainted from a sudden blow, he smiled sadly and nodded, mouthing her name. Even when her eyes closed, all she could see was the dead stillness in his eyes.

Mariya awoke what seemed like hours later. The sun had set a long time ago, and the now the moon took its place in the sky. With a blink, Mariya sat up and looked at the moon. If she died, her life would be fully ruled by it. The vampire blood in her veins would take over and she would never see the sun again. She shivered under its icy glow, feeling its power within her. It made her blood run cold, like ice flooded through her and stole her breath.

Mariya was still fighting the nightcrawler inside of her,

51

the mystic abilities that awaited her in the moonlight. Mariya didn't want that, though; she hated the darkness and was afraid of it. She was scared to let go. She hated being alone.

But that's what the life of a vampire was all about.

It was a cursed life, a path ridden with the blood of her victims and the kinsmen before her. It was horrid to her, and she didn't enjoy it one bit. Of course, she didn't ask for any of this. She was part vampire at birth and it was wrong. She shouldn't have existed. Vampires and humankind usually didn't have children, yet here she was.

A miracle in the darkness.

With a groan, she got to her feet and straightened out her skirt. This world seemed odd to her, the night. The sights and sounds were all startling, and yet exciting and inviting at the same time. It all welcomed her, tried to get her to dance with the stars and to bask in the beauty of the moon. Mariya resisted the pull, though, and forced herself to keep walking along the dirt path.

Yet, the magic proved to be too much.

She forgot her fear and let herself be enveloped by the wondrous mysteries around her. There was a feeling of giddiness that spread quickly through her, making her blood run hot. Never before had she felt this alive. And with a laugh, she gave into the ache of her muscles and took off running.

Laughing surrounded him, the sights and sounds of the

bar closing in on the young man. One of his friends playfully slapped him on the back, hard. Esiviel grimaced and took another sip of his drink.

He sat in the darkest corner of the bar possible, watching everything that transpired. It was always like this. Esiviel was barely one hundred, but already bored with his life. It saddened him, but he often reminded himself that this was the life of a nightcrawler. With a sigh, Esiviel closed his eyes and hummed a hymn he remembered from long ago:

Far away from the land I see,

The winds carry me tonight

On a silken shore,

My lover waits for me,

To hold me close

His thoughts were interrupted when someone who looked like a teenage girl sat next him. Her hair was a jet black that reflected the strata of colors from the lights of the club. Her almost hazel eyes were shaded by unkept bangs and she always looked down.

She quietly called the bartender and ordered a small glass of cheep brandy. It was probably meant to take the edge of reality away from awhile. Her eyes were ringed by black circles and her arms were littered with blue and black bruises, some edged with a deep red circle. With a nod, the bartender smiled at her and turned to fill her order. "Aren't you a little young to be drinking?" Esiviel questioned, looking at her with sympathy.

The girl cautiously looked over at him and Esiviel gasped. She had eyes like his, they were hollow. Hers sparkled with the promise of life, but were shaded by the shadow of death just around the corner. "No, why?"

Esiviel took a deep breath and regained himself, "I couldn't help but notice your eyes. . ."

The girl's eyes flashed a brilliant green and she tensed, "Who are you?!" She demanded.

Esiviel put his hands up in submission, "Sorry, just a question." He sighed, "The name's Esiviel Colombain."

The girl calmed down and nodded, "Mariya Gallion."

Esiviel nodded in acknowledgment, "So, what's the story?"

"Huh?" Mariya jumped and almost fell off the barstool out of surprise.

Esiviel quickly caught her and helped her to her feet. Mariya pulled away abruptly, a blush running across her pale, bruise littered face. "Like I would tell someone I just met," she snapped.

Esiviel sighed, She's just like The Council said she would be. Yet, I wouldn't expect a girl like her to be next in line for the throne. He shrugged and looked at the ceiling, "I guess you're right, but let me tell you this: You're not alone."

Mariya looked at him oddly and sat back down slowly, "What do you mean?"

Esiviel looked back down at his glass and tilted it in various directions, watching the light reflect off the polished

54

crystal. "I can sense it in you, it's weak, but definitely there. You hide it though, you're afraid of the moon and don't know how to surrender your soul to her. And yet," he sighed, "You wish to be among the living, even though the sun will soon reject your bleeding heart. Am I right?"

Mariya blinked in surprise. Who was this man? How did he know about her blood? Subconsciously, she put her hand over her pounding heart, "How did. . .?"

Before she could utter a complete sentence, she felt strong arms around her. In an instant, a frigid rush chilled her to the core of her very existence. This person was not of the living, the world no longer could pass judgement on his soul or even see him as part of the ever changing fibers of life. He was of pure blood.

Dead.

"I keep telling you, my dear," Esiviel whispered gently in her ear, "I'm just like you, we're the same."

Mariya almost immediately froze up, feeling his cool breath against her skin. A blush ran across her pale face, painting it red. It was just like the mist she used, but she was a vampire! Surely she couldn't fall for her own tricks. Suddenly her eyes widened and the force of her sudden realization felt as if someone had punched her.

Pleasure.

Desire for something beyond the feed.

Mariya closed her eyes gently and tried to clear her thoughts. She couldn't be weak, she had to resist. Yet, her heart pulled her into the emotions she never had felt before. It tried to plunge her into a world beyond the icy blackness she had grown accustomed to.

"Esiviel. . ." Mariya breathed, embarrassed that her breath was so hot, and tired to wiggle out of his embrace as if she dreaded the rush that his touch brought.

"Hush, little one, I will not harm you. I'll always be watching and waiting for you, my dear, just as I always have been and always will. Watch yourself," he whispered passionately and kissed the arch of her neck. Almost as quick as he had appeared, he let go and blended into the shadows.

Gone.

"Esiviel!" Mariya turned quickly in hopes to catch him before he disappeared. Yet, he was long gone, although she still felt his presence.

Death.

Chills.

With a dejected sigh, Mariya turned back to her drink. After a taking a small sip, barely enough to coat the tongue, she let her hand subconsciously brush where Esiviel had kissed her. They had just met, hadn't they? If they had, then why did Mariya feel as if she had known him all of her miserable existence? It made no sense, and her mind raced trying to figure it out. She had melted away at his touch, and she almost did again when she flashed back to the memory of that swift pang shooting through her. Mariya had yearned for it for so long. Could he really understand her?

*She sighed dejectedly, remembering a song from when
she was a child:*

> *I'm still running in my dreams,*
>
> *even when it hurts too much*
>
> *I can see you there,*
>
> *watching me*
>
> *Yet I still let go,*
>
> *and into my abyss.*

*Could it really mean something? Trying to shake off the
newly awakened emotions, Mariya lost herself in thought. She
was learning to live, although she had died long ago. No, it
couldn't happen. She was to be queen, she couldn't lose herself
in such affairs. Never, it wasn't acceptable. Yet, her resolve
dissipated at the remembrance of the heat that spread over her
the second his lips touched her skin.*

*Confused, Mariya slipped out of the bar with her head
full of so many thoughts. Even the persistent buzz of the night
had been silenced, at least it seemed like it. This couldn't be
real.*

It shouldn't be.

6. How Long Is Forever?

Mariya forced herself to get up. After getting dressed, she quickly brushed out her mane of hair and dug under her bed for her ballet flats. That particular morning seemed odd, off somehow. Yes, it was still early and it was likely that Ivy and Deryk were still asleep, but not even Scout ran to greet her in the living room like usual. The entire house was silent, like the environment had been thrown into a deep slumber. Mariya just shrugged it off, she was just worked up over the recent murders. It had to be her imagination playing tricks on her, her mind was still focused on Esiviel's disappearance.

That's what she thought.

59

She could tell something was amiss the second she stepped foot in the living room. The room seemed twisted and horribly distorted. It was as if someone had thrown the room into a blender and pureed it. Mariya paused curiously at the bookshelves, looking over the many photos that occupied any available room. Absentmindedly, she pieced everything together.

The air in the room was heavy, stagnant. For a moment, Mariya found it hard to breathe, as if the air itself was energy. She closed her eyes and calmed down, then opened them to find the pictures had no faces; they had been erased in the span of three seconds. Sighing, she drew in a deep breath and gagged. The air was like that of a morgue, it smelled heavily of death. A bile rose in her throat as the scent became so strong she could almost taste it. Swallowing her disgust, Mariya picked up one of the frames.

Almost instantly, she dropped it again with a shriek of surprise. The edges had been sharpened to a point, much like that of a blade. The glass hit the floor at top speed, but didn't make a sound as it shattered and covered the ground in a carpet of diamond-like shards. Innocently, Mariya pressed her bleeding finger to her lips in hopes she could stop the flow of blood. She whimpered, then the hairs on the back of her neck stood up.

She wasn't alone.

Mariya froze, not even daring to take a breath. She didn't move an inch out of fear, maybe hoping that if she stayed still she would not be seen. But she knew it was too late. They, or it, was here for her. With a blink, her eyes grew wide in horrified recognition. She knew this aura all too well, and with it came an overwhelming sense of dread and hatred.

It was her father.

Mariya sharply turned to face her unwelcome visitor, her skirt flaring out to compliment the smoldering hatred in her eyes. For a moment, her eyes flashed forest green and her heartbeat picked up when adrenaline flushed through her.

"Ah, Mariya!" Her father greeted her calmly, holding out his arms as if to embrace her.

Mariya balled her hands into fists at her sides and flared her aura in response. "What do you want?" She asked angrily, her voice dripping icicles.

Her father sighed calmly and picked up one of the frames, looking at it with a bored expression. His dark hair fell in front of his face and hid the bit of envy that grew in his eyes. "It's sad," he started with a sigh, "Associating with these humans and trying to hide your true nature."

Mariya shoved his comment aside, "He'd better alive, Devon."

Her father put the frame down with a bored expression, "Who? Your worthless mate?" He looked at Mariya with a sinister grin and an evil spark in his eye,

"You never know. . ." He took a step toward Mariya.

Mariya tensed, taking a step back and bracing herself in case the worst happened. Devon took another step, looking like he enjoyed the silent torture. He knew the fact he was here scared Mariya senseless, and relished the chance to control her. Then he walked past, no walked *through* her. Mariya shivered, as if a breeze had blown over her. The coldness of death embraced her, and she closed her eyes as if wishing it away but images incomprehensibly washed through her mind.

Bodies.

Rivers of blood.

Death, everywhere.

Seemingly endless madness.

Mariya was about to open her eyes again when an unseen force grabbed her and pulled her down into a darkness not the even the moon could light.

Mariya was falling, or at least that's what it felt like. She looked up and saw life slipping by, much like a falling angel would. Flashes of her past were all around her, as if someone were playing videos of her most intimate thoughts. She watched as her birth, meeting Esiviel, meeting Ivy, and even her mother's death replayed themselves right before her eyes. She looked straight up, and tilted her head as if someone was trying to rip her heart from her chest.

With a solid squeeze, the force grew stronger. It kept pulling, yanking, at her until it let go and threw her to the ground. Mariya hit the ground with a hard thud, and for a while, she lay where she fell. All the air in her was forced out with such a great intensity that she shook violently and gasped like a fish out of water. Even when she did manage to catch her breath, it was stolen from her again as if someone had a vacuum to her lips. She closed her eyes and curled her hands into fists, feeling the moist grass beneath her.

Mariya panted shallowly, and she finally managed to get air into her lungs and keep it there. Taking a deep breath, she tensed slightly and forced herself to sit up. Looking around, she rubbed her back and tried to calm her racing mind. Mariya was sitting in a field, stretching as far as she could see. On the horizon to her left, there was a misshapen shadowy ridge that looked like mountains. With what seemed like a grunt, Mariya forced herself to her feet and stretched.

She closed her eyes for a moment, and felt like the world was spinning so fast it shook her off balance. Almost immediately, Mariya opened her eyes again and righted herself.

What in Hell's name? Mariya thought, rubbing her head and looking around.

Her mind registered everything around her, but nothing made sense or was even vaguely familiar. A sense of dread washed over her, but she forced it back down and tried to gather all of her inner strength. Mariya shook a little as she took her first step, her hands slipping out of her tight fists because of sweaty palms.

Instantly, the grass around her foot, or rather the entire field, shriveled into a lifeless wasteland. The azure sky turned a velvety purple, the clouds a pale pink. Mariya looked around frantically, trying to get a grip on the situation. Out of the corner of her eye, she saw a movement. Focusing her gaze on the movement in the grass, she drew in a gasp and her eyes grew wide in horrific realization.

Crimson flowed from under Mariya's slippered foot. First a small stream that wove its way through the flakes and strands of brown, then more soon joined it and formed a river that flowed straight from Mariya. Numbly, Mariya's eyes followed the trail to a dark pile of various sized lumps. Swallowing the bile in her throat, she gingerly walked up to the pile.

Corpses.

Dozens of them.

They were piled on top of another, all their faces frozen in the same expression of uncomprehending horror.

You did this, Mariya heard a voice thunder. *It's your fault they're dead.*

Mariya shook her head as if to say 'no', but didn't

move her eyes from the grisly pile. She couldn't have done this. She couldn't have. The elders always told her not to kill, no matter how sweet the blood was or how badly her body called for it. Killing was wrong. Mariya went to ball her hands into fists again, but they slipped. There was a fluid running down her wrists like a spider web, connecting at her palm, then separating again and dripping off her fingers.

Blood.

Mariya gasped and suppressed a scream, holding her hands away from her as if that would make it stop. She took a deep breath and then realized it was flowing from a deep wound in her shoulder. Pain racked Mariya's body, sending a series of tremors running through her. Her lips grew pale and thin as her life force joined the rivers of the others. A shallow, rasping breath entered her, barely passing her lips.

You must bleed with them as well, the voice came again, *and die with them.*

The world narrowed to a tunnel as her eyes fluttered to tiny slits. She heard the voices of the bodies, all asking her the same thing. *Why?* They blamed her for this, telling her she could have stopped him and put an end to the terror. She silently apologized to the world as the ground rose up from beneath her. A sudden force hit her and she was looking at the sky, lying on her back. Her body grew limp as the gods pulled her from her suffering and right there in that desecrated field, Mariya Gallion the half-vampire died.

Mariya blinked in the afternoon light and looked up to see young eyes looking down at her through a line of tears. She smiled weakly at Ivy and tried to hold back the bile that rose up in her throat as she sat up.

"Sissy, are you okay?" Ivy asked innocently.

Mariya nodded, "I'm fine, Ivy." Her voice came out as a hoarse whisper, not giving the encouraging effect she had hoped for.

The vision, or whatever it was, troubled her. She had never experienced a vision before, and she wondered why it started now. She felt dizzy, as if the world was spinning faster than usual and throwing her off balance. Mariya also felt hollow, but pained at the same time. She closed her eyes to take a deep breath and swirls of black and red flashed in her, spreading a feeling of intense hatred through her. She flinched outwardly, and Ivy cocked her head curiously. Mariya knew this wasn't her and explored it. A moan escaped her throat when she brushed the energy, but she pushed even further. After hesitating for a moment, she plunged in completely with a scream that pierced the heavens.

The feeling was intense, relentless. A sweat broke out on Mariya's brow as she tried to pull back but realized she couldn't.

"Sissy!' Ivy screamed and took Mariya's hand in hers.

Mariya's hand was cold, clammy. Her heartbeat steadily slowed until it was barely existent. Her breathing became harsh, each breath harder than the last. And eventually, it stopped altogether. Yet, she didn't feel dead. In fact, somehow she felt alive, so alive. Her blood burned, feeling like fire running through her veins and trying to swallow her alive.

Mariya fell back again, the usual pain of hitting the floor numbed completely. She desperately yanked away from the contact, pulling away as if she were an animal with its foot caught in a trap. Part of her knew that she could die, and that's all her instincts yelled at her.

Fight it!

She gasped for breath, but stopped when something yelled at her not to. Mariya didn't know why she was listening so obediently to a voice she had never heard before. Maybe it wasn't even a voice, it was the animalistic instincts to live inside of every living thing. Whatever it was, Mariya was compelled to listen without question. The small of ether of resistance in her disappeared, pulling her into a half-dead trance.

Footsteps echoed somewhere far off, followed closely by anxious shouting. Someone placed a hand on her shoulder, and the contact felt like torture. She whimpered, trying to pull away but realizing she couldn't control her own body. Someone whispered her name, trying to call her back from the other side. She drew in a shuddering breath in response, an icy rush chilling her.

Mariya felt someone press a hand into her chest, right where her breastbone ended. It was calm for a moment, as if time had froze. The person whispered some kind of chant in Latin and a tingling sensation spread through her, making her feel pins and needles everywhere. She was thrown into a bright light, and she tensed as if she was bracing herself for the worse but the expected pain never came.

The person chanting stopped and gently whispered, "It's over, Mariya. Calm down."

Mariya drew in a deep breath, but was forced into a bank of the hottest flames. She screamed in both body and spirit, feeling the otherworldly heat that threatened to overtake her. Her chest hurt, as if someone had gripped her heart and was pulling her to the heavens. A single tear rolled down her cheek in the physical plane before she woke up.

Mariya woke suddenly, gasping wildly. A cold sweat ran down her face, making her feel like someone had splashed her with a cool glass of water. Her heart raced, pounding as if it wanted to break free of her chest. For a moment, she just closed her eyes and caught her breath, trying to calm her hyperactive body. After gathering up what was left of her, she bit her lip and sat up.

Mariya looked over to see Kristopher, smiling broadly at her with a concerned twinkle in his eye. Ivy stood behind him, her hands clutched tightly together, her bright blue eyes clouded with worry. Another girl stood beside Kristopher, slightly younger than Ivy. Her brown hair fell in front of her eyes in a ratty fashion, barely hiding the brown eyes beneath the unkept bangs. She was dressed in a tank top and checkered skirt that was stitched up one side. She looked at Mariya over the edge of a wooden board that she tightly clutched to her chest.

"What happened?" Mariya asked weakly, rubbing her aching head.

"It was a small grade possession," the little girl spoke up, "The person was trying to kill you."

Mariya froze, mouthing her father's name. "How?" She asked absentmindedly.

Kristopher sighed. "Thank you, Anna-Marie," he looked at the girl standing next to him. He looked at Mariya, "And Mariya, spiritual death is worse than physical."

"But how could my *soul* die?"

The girl called Anna-Marie stamped her foot impatiently, a hand on her hip. "You could die on the inside! And you could stay like forever. Never know anything else, either. All you would know is pain!"

"You mean Sissy wouldn't go to heaven?" Ivy asked, walking over to kneel next to Mariya who slipped an arm around her shoulders comfortingly.

Kristopher nodded solemnly, "Exactly. She'd be tortured for eternity."

He was inside me, Mariya thought, her shaking hand clutching the shirt over her heart. *He knows everything.*

A shiver rippled up her spine, wishing Esiviel was there like normal to hold her in his arms and fight her fears away. He always did, he helped her feel sane even in the tightest situations, but now she was alone.

Alone.

A haze of helplessness filled her eyes and she looked up as if she could see the sky through the ceiling. The warmth of the sun from the window surrounded her, and she soaked up the warmth like life. Mariya closed her eyes and focused, searching for Esiviel's energy signature in a way she had grown accustomed to. She always did this when they were apart, communicate with him telepathically. Any vampire, or any person in general, could. All they needed was to be mentally strong and deeply bonded or familiar with the person they were trying to reach.

She found him, and quickly grabbed a hold of the presence. She found her inner, true, voice and focused her thoughts. *Esiviel, please hold on. . .*

It was dark all around him. The usually calming shadows seemed threatening, even the most serene thing wouldn't help him now. His head hurt, and it was excruciatingly painful to try to focus his vision. He tried to move, but his hands were bound by a thick chain. Esiviel pushed back, and felt a steel pipe behind him, probably what the chain was wrapped around. Even though the pipe was starting to rust, it was nothing he could break free of.

After calming down, he took a careful catalogue of his injuries. His trench coat had been torn off, leaving his lacerated arms exposed. For a moment, Esiviel could barely see any skin beneath the dried blood and cuts that covered him. The whole right side of his face hurt and by the feel of it, he could tell it was going to turn into a giant bruise. One eye wanted to swell shut, but he forced it to stay open.

Esiviel sighed and hummed a single note. He paused, listening for the echoes. By his guess, it was about the size of a small storehouse. Puzzled, he closed his eyes and sat back for a moment and almost dozed off. Fighting it off, he shook his head and sat up straight. Then, Esiviel thought he heard someone call his name. He instantly snapped to attention.

"Hello?" He called, his voice raspy.

Yet only the sound of his own voice echoed back to him. With a sigh, he leaned back again, confused. Then he understood. He closed his eyes and opened his mind, completely letting go of reality. There, in a world between, he was surrounded by the most comforting light. Once again, the voice gently called to him, his name echoing through the abyss.

"Esiviel. . ."

"Who's there?" He asked, looking around nervously.

"Behind you," the person whispered and he turned to see Mariya standing behind him. Her eyes gleamed helplessly, begging forgiveness.

From him.

"Please hang on, okay?" Her gentle voice was soft, so soft it seemed like she was whispering in his ear. "Just wait for me."

A shock went through him, "I'd wait forever."

Mariya nodded, then hung her head shamefully. "I'm so sorry, love. It's all my fault you got stuck in this mess. My father only wants me. He wants to kill me."

"Why?"

Mariya shrugged, as if the thought of her own death didn't bother her, "Who knows?" She sighed, "Fear perhaps."

Esiviel flinched in both essence and reality. He knew exactly why they were hunted over and over. It was fear that caused Devon to chase them, fear of his own daughter. The truth was, Mariya was powerful but she hid it. She refused to touch her magic abilities, although she was gifted. It scared her. Esiviel had felt it, back when he first kissed her. That's what made him pull back so quickly, the energies she kept hidden within her.

It all comes back to fear.

"Mariya," his voice grew cautious, "Watch yourself."

"Why?" She looked at him oddly, *"You're* the one that's hurt."

"Because Devon. . ."

The contact slipped, and the images went static like a satellite image in a storm. Esiviel struggled to keep a hold on it, but the ether slipped from both him *and* Mariya. He opened his eyes suddenly when a strong force struck him in the stomach.

The right side of his face hurt and blood trickled down his cheek from his temple. His eyes flashed out of fear, then he made the mistake of looking up. His eyes met green ones, similar to Mariya's when changed. Esiviel's entire body tensed and he froze, not even daring to move his eyes the slightest.

"Hello, Esiviel," the person smiled with mock sincerity, "How nice to see you." Esiviel remained silent, bracing himself for whatever was coming next. The person continued, acting like it was a casual conversation and ignored Esiviel's glares of intense hatred. "Missing your Mariya? Don't worry, she's not hurt. But I need you. You see, your dear Mariya is. . ."

"Stronger than you," Esiviel interjected, then

immediately bit his tongue. *Oops.* But he shrugged it off and sat up confidently, his eyes glowing with admiration for his mate. "You're afraid of her, Devon. You know that she can beat you even though she's only of half-blood."

Devon whirled, and Esiviel winced as Devon smacked his already pounding head hard, "Never say that!" Devon growled, "That filthy half-blood could never beat me. Ever."

Esiviel grinned and ignored the pulsing pain, "So you fight her. You're not any better than any human. You run from her, in a way, and fight her to hide your fear."

"You're right there," Devon grinned evilly, reaching into his back pocket. "Have you heard about the murders?"

"You did that," Esiviel spat, "You don't know what Mariya's like nowadays so you're weeding her out by killing all those innocent teens." He sighed and looked at Devon in disgust, his eyes tiny slits, "And then you frame her."

Esiviel saw a flash of silver, then felt an exploding pain in his already sore shoulder. He drew in a shuddering breath, and forced himself to sit tall. Devon leaned in close, "And you will help me find her." He twisted the knife and drove it deeper into Esiviel's shoulder.

Esiviel screamed out in pain, the sound of his agony echoing back to him. His breath grew even more labored, as he met Devon's eyes while trying to put all the hate in

74

him into his nearly colorless eyes. "Go to Hell," he spat, struggling against the blade, but only succeeding in driving it deeper into his shoulder.

"I'm sorry it hurts, but I need your help," Devon teased, pressing the blade even farther in until Esiviel could hear it scrape against the wall behind him.

"Never," he wheezed, clenching his teeth. *It's all for you, Mariya. . .*

"Oh, but you will help," Devon teased and ripped the blade out quickly, making Esiviel scream out again. Devon grinned at his prisoner's pain, and his smile turned menacing, "Or I'll kill you slowly and *both* of you will suffer."

Mariya paused and looked over shoulder, swearing she heard someone call her name. It was like someone screamed it at her with all their heart, but it was still gentle. It was full of sympathy and flowed like a quiet brook; silent and yet still noticed.

"He needs you," Anna-Marie mused from across the table.

Mariya turned back to the girl sitting across from her. Anna-Marie's eyes were closed, focused on the pendulum hanging from her hand. There was Ouija board on the table in front of her, and Anna-Marie would occasionally mouth a question to it. It wasn't kid version either, it was really controlled by spirits. And Anna-

Marie's clairvoyance made it work even better. It would prove to be a valuable tool for Mariya, if she was to find her mate or even fight her father.

With a sigh, Mariya watched the prism swing freely on the chain. The silver glittered in the light, throwing a rainbow of colors against the wall. The rainbow danced in every direction, reflecting the afternoon's glorious warmth throughout the room. It all danced and twinkled with the motion of the chain, appearing and disappearing with each swing of the prism.

"What do you mean?" Mariya questioned, looking at Anna-Marie oddly.

"He's dying," Anna went on, her voice hollow because of her trance. "But he wills himself to keep going just for you."

"Idiot," Mariya muttered, closing her eyes with a knowing smile. *Let go,* she thought, her eyes tearing. *Don't hold on for me.*

Anna sighed impatiently, "Mariya! This will only work if you pay attention!"

"Sorry. . ." Mariya muttered and looked up at Anna-Marie.

"They say we -Daddy and I- have to help you, teach you. They also say there will be two tragedies soon. One will kill someone you hold very dear. The other. . ." Anna was suddenly pulled out of her trance. Her eyes teared guiltily and she buried her face in her hands. "I'm so sorry,

Mariya." She shook her head as if willing away a nightmare, her small form shaking uncontrollably.

Kristopher sighed and gathered her up in his arms, shushing her gently. He looked at Mariya questioningly, but got nothing. Mariya's eyes were frozen wide, the color drained from them. They were completely hollow in pure innocence. Anna dropped the pendulum and it shattered in what seemed like an explosion of shards. Promptly, she threw her arms around Kristopher's neck, still crying wildly. With a sigh, Kristopher picked her up and held her tight, still shushing her. Over his shoulder, he looked at Mariya, his eyes daring her to say something.

Anything.

Why?

Mariya stared numbly at the shards of bloodstone that littered the floor and table. For a moment, the crimson stone seemed to melt and pour over the edges of the table.

Abruptly, Mariya was in a candle-lit room and a gravelly voice called her name. She felt someone touch her shoulder, as if to pull her into something. Mariya quickly willed the vision away, shaking her head to clear her mind.

It didn't clear.

It became more vibrant.

The white walls of the room melted away, turning into cobblestone. 'Look up,' something told her and she mechanically obeyed.

There was a small body on the table in front of her. It was a little girl, neatly arranged on her back as if she was being prepped for a funeral ceremony. And as Mariya's vision adjusted to the light she saw it was flayed.

The skin was completely cut off the chest of the girl, showing all of her innards. The heart still beat and with every pump more blood spilled onto the table. It flowed down the legs of the table, almost like a river, and formed grisly pools on the floor at Mariya's feet. As Mariya rose from the wicker chair she sat in, her feet dipped into the crimson pools and she grimaced. Usually she would have gagged or turned away by now, but there was nowhere to turn to. The entire room smelt of death, it had an aura all of its own. No, instead she tried to get better view of the girl's face. As soon as she saw the wisps of blonde hair, she staggered backwards and her breath caught in her throat.

Tripping over the tails of her skirt, she fell backwards. Mariya awkwardly caught herself on her hands, only to find herself lying in her loved one's blood. It seemed to soak through her stained clothes, to go right to Mariya's soul. It was becoming part of her, this death becoming one of the many in her life as a vampiress. It went right through her, settling in her bones and washing over her consciousness.

Baptism of death.

Gathering herself, Mariya willed her racing heart to calm and took a deep breath. With a grimace, she forced herself to her feet. The pale white of her skin was now dyed pink. It was with her forever. Swallowing harshly, she looked back at the girl with the blood rushing in her ears.

It was Ivy.

Her platinum blonde was plastered to her sweat soaked face. Her bangs looked more like strawberry blonde, the blood crusted on her face making the scene even more grim. She still struggled to hold onto life, panting as if her failing lungs could really save her. She fought for dear life, although her eyes showed she was already crossing the gate.

"Sissy. . ." she weakly called out, her eyes losing all color.

'This isn't real.' Mariya thought to herself, 'It can't be.' Swallowing the bile in her throat, Mariya walked over and took Ivy's small hand in hers. "I'm here sweetie," she whispered, although she knew Ivy couldn't -and wouldn't- ever hear her.

Slowly, the flow of blood stopped, and formed a small trickle. Mariya shook, knowing what it meant as Ivy rasped for her last breath then lay still. She paused, almost like she could deny that this was real. Shaking her head, Mariya accepted the truth she saw in Ivy's lifeless blue eyes. With a saddened sigh and a choked sob, Mariya swept her spare hand over Ivy's eyes to close them.

It was over.

Kristopher put the still sniffling Anna-Marie down carefully. "Mariya?" he gently put his hand on her shoulder.

Bang!

Mariya was pulled out of her trance suddenly, her eyes wide. They shined with the brilliance of pure fear, a trait she still shared with her human side. She blinked and looked at Kristopher questioningly, her hazel eyes flashing forest green. Nothing made sense anymore. Nothing.

Merely a week earlier, she was a normal vampiress. Now? Now, she wasn't sure what she was. She was sure that she didn't like it though. She didn't like the energies inside her. Closing her eyes to hide the frustrated tears, she shook her head in disbelief. It was all too much, everything.

"I'm going for a walk," she mumbled as she stood up and stretched.

"Mariya!" Kristopher called after her.

"Please, Kristopher, I just want to be alone," she faintly whispered, weakly leaning on the frame of the front door.

"Mariya, I know this is a lot, but you have to accept that things have changed. It. . ." Kristopher tired to explain, his voice gentle.

"No!" Mariya snapped. "I was normal just days before this! Now I'm some. . ." She paused, "Freak!" With

80

a smothered scream of anger, she flung the door open and ran into the inviting chill of the night.

The angered disk of fire was slowly disappearing behind the hills. It answered the moon's calls, giving up its daytime kingdom for the peace of night. The gray storm clouds turned purple in its glow, splashing against the vibrant reds on the gods' canvas. The earth was silent in anticipation of what was being promised by the masses of cotton in the sky. There was such a peaceful feel, even the air smelling sweet with excitement. But still Mariya ran as if she could escape what she was becoming.

Her feet carried to her to the very club where she and Esiviel met. It was a popular hole-in-the-wall hang out for local vampires, and the thought of it seemed so inviting. As soon as she opened the rusty door to the two room brick building she was bathed in the bright lights of the dance floor. The loud and rowdy music wrapped around her, making her feel like what happened back at the house was nothing.

Music that pulls at the heart, she thought happily, closing the rustic door behind her.

Trying to avoid running into anyone, Mariya carefully made her way across the floor. She felt uneasy under the stares of her people. A few even bowed their heads to her, and she simply smiled in response. One even recited an old blessing.

May your fangs never dull.

They knew, and accepted, her as their queen. Their *real* queen. And it worried her. What if she wasn't able to live up to their expectations? She was pulled out of her thoughts by a young blond who caught her by the arm. Smiling warmly, Mariya immediately recognized the young half-blood. His blond hair fell in front of uncustomarily bright eyes that looked at her with a sheen of worry.

"Hello, Sathir," she greeted him, bowing her head in acknowledgment and sat at the table with him.

Sathir used to be a student of Esiviel's, but was passed onto Zethin when she and Esiviel fled the kingdom. He was dragged into his afterlife after being blooded by a rogue vampire. Like usual, he favored his mineral washed blue jeans and leather biker jacket. No shirt.

She paused, a scowl forming on her face when she noticed the look in the young vampire's eyes. "What's wrong?"

"I was about to ask *you* the same thing," he countered in his normal laid back tone of voice. She had to strain to listen, just because his voice was naturally quiet.

Mariya sighed sadly and her eyes grew vacant. "Esiviel has gone missing."

A pained look spread across Sathir's face. "Figured as much. Any idea who did it?"

Mariya looked around the room uneasily, then

turned back to Sathir. In a voice so quiet she didn't think she said anything, she whispered, "My father."

The air in the room grew heavy, and everything seemed to be silenced. A few of the faces at the tables near them looked at Mariya in horror, their gazes piercing her faintly beating heart. She hated to see her people like that. But fear also struck, what if her power was rejected and she couldn't take her place on the throne? No, that wouldn't happen. She had legend on her side.

Sathir sighed, ignoring the stares and whispers in his usual manner. "Figured as much. Why's he after Esiviel?"

"He's after me," Mariya whispered as hushed discussions resumed around them, "He knows Esiviel's my weak point."

"And?"

"He's trying to find me, kill me." As Mariya said those words, she finally understood what it meant and what was happening. "He's afraid of me," Mariya whispered, her eyes widening in sudden realization. "Of my power and what I can become." The words seemed like she was more thinking out loud then talking to Sathir. Her voice was hollow, betraying the confusion in her mind.

"And he's jealous," A new, elderly voice joined in, "Of our soon-to-be leader. And what can happen."

"Zethin!" Mariya shouted excitedly, hugging her old mentor like a small child would their mother.

Zethin laughed and patted her on the head, "Easy, little one. I'm not what I used to be."

Mariya beamed and pulled back, studying the effect the years had on him. He seemed frail like a leaf, skinny and tall but Mariya knew otherwise. Back in his prime, he would give Mariya beat downs and teach her the sweet art of fighting. During her grandmother's rule, he was Captain of the royal guard and was even the late Queen Rosa's trusted bodyguard. His once dark hair was now faded at the roots, and his awkwardly colored eyes seemed like they were clouding over.

Sathir smiled warmly and teasingly mocked, "What? Can't I go to town without being stalked by my teacher?" After a disapproving glare from Mariya, he laughed uneasily, "Teasing." Sathir quickly regained his composure, "Please, join us."

The elderly vampire smiled and sat at the table with them, his eyes studying Mariya carefully. Sathir continued, "Zethin, what do you mean by 'Mariya's royalty'?"

"I left that life a long time ago," Mariya interjected before her former teacher could say anything. Her eyes glowed with hatred at the memories of the royal family. "The family's all snobs anyway."

"You're still next in line for the throne, Mariya Annette. You're the rightful queen."

"I know," she grumbled then straightened herself up

in mock confidence, "But they already have Rosabella's mom on the throne in my place. . .why would they need me?"

"She's only your stand in. You know the Council really wants you. Besides, you're the vampire in the legend," Zethin corrected her.

Sathir's jaw went slack, "You mean the prophecy?!"

Mariya sighed and in a bored tone recited the legend. She closed her eyes and her beautifully peaceful voice betrayed her act:

In the time of greatest horror, a phoenix will rise from the ashes. Born from the blood of a human mistress and one of full blood, a life will begin under the guidance of the goddess. Her name shall be pure, and all will know it. It will be whispered on the wind on her arrival, but none shall hear it. Great power will soon come and an age of hope shall begin for all.

Sathir smiled admirably at her, settling back in his chair as she finished the tale:

It is up to those who guard her to deliver her unto her destiny. Only then will the land be silenced and peace will fall upon all.

Mariya sighed, "But that could be anyone." She pointed out in a whisper and opened her eyes, "That story is thousands of years old! Plus, there's many of dirty blood in this world. Not just me."

Zethin sighed, "But nevertheless, you were raised as

any other vampiric child would be. They didn't want you to feel different."

"Too late," Mariya grumbled, her brow furrowed with a scowl.

"What do you mean, my dear?" Zethin looked at his former student with fatherly love in his eyes.

Mariya looked at her hands in guilt, "I've been having odd visions about the murders that have been happening." She looked away, her eyes filled with tears, "And my powers have reawakened."

Sathir looked between Mariya and Zethin nervously, "But didn't they seal those away?"

Zethin nodded in agreement and looked Mariya directly in her eyes. "You must have come in contact with something of a much higher power." His tone was even, but his eyes pierced through her, daring her to admit it. He wanted to admit that she had been possessed and was now tortured every time she closed her eyes.

She sighed, "My father. . .visited." Subconsciously, her hand tightly clutched the shirt over her heart. Both of the others stayed quiet but the look in their eyes told her to continue. "I was. . .possessed by the ethereal presence of Devon. He tried to kill me, he really did. I felt his hate. . .everything. . .but. . ." She stopped suddenly as if she had just remembered something. "Fear. There was an intense fear. He was trying to hide it. . .but it was painfully obvious."

Zethin looked at Mariya oddly, "How do you..?"

Like once before, she suddenly snapped back to reality. This time, she heard a scream. Her scream. She was calling Esiviel's name as if her life depended on it. Screaming with all her heart and soul. Mariya looked around the room oddly, looking like she woke up in a place different than she was before.

Sathir caught it, "Mariya, you slipped there."

Mariya nodded, but stopped short when something tugged at her.

Screaming.

Crying.

Calling her.

There was a darkness that gradually faded into a deep crimson. The haze cleared and she choked down a gasp of shock. Esiviel was being beaten, torn. Her father kept stabbing, slapping, kicking, torturing him.

But he never let go.

Esiviel fought hard to stay in touch with reality, but his outward appearance was deceiving.

He was scared.

He was crying on the inside.

Death was there, he felt it.

In his mind, he apologized to Mariya over and over again. The only reason for him to hold on echoed in her mind repeatedly. The only reason for the pain she felt in her chest.

I love her.

87

She trusts me.

I can't let her down.

Mariya tensed as once again a dagger was shoved through Esiviel's chest but he didn't even let out a scream of pain. Then a mist covered her.

Fog.

Death.

The image fogged and hazed. It dissolved before her like alka-seltzer in water. Then a sudden pain hit her. Her pain, no one else's. It was a sharp pain in her back. She could tell it was a blade, but she didn't know the assailant. There was a hoarse whisper that called her name. The person's breath on her cheek made her skin crawl, then she saw him.

Her father.

"Long live the queen," he whispered mockingly then disappeared into the gray abyss.

Somewhere far away she heard Esiviel ask, "Why?"

But she didn't have an answer.

"Mariya!" Sathir shouted, shaking her shoulder.

Something like a moan escaped her throat. Mariya dropped her head into her hands and rubbed her temples as if she had a headache.

"What happened?" Sathir asked, his voice shaking, "You stopped breathing."

Mariya mutely shook her head sadly just as a tear rolled down her cheek. It was too much, all of it. She was in over her head now, and she wanted out.

Now.

"I can't take this. . ." She muttered weakly, shaking.

"What..?" Sathir started to comfort, "Take what?"

"Any of this!" Mariya cried angrily, "It's all too big, too much. A week ago, everything was fine. . .Now. . ." her voice grew broken and hoarse, "Everyone, everything, I hold dear is in danger. . ." Her voice trailed off in a sob but she shuddered through it, "Because of. . .because of me." Her voice fully cracked and she hid her face in her hands, not wanting anyone to see her like this. Mariya's dark hair fell over like a veil and covered her, hiding her from the world's eye.

Sathir sighed and reached out to gently rub Mariya's shoulder, but he was pushed back by a barrier. He recoiled, a shout of surprise escaping his lips. All of her bottled up emotions had spilled over and separated her from the world, forming a psychic shield around her.

She was alone now.

Just like she wanted.

Falling.

Gracefully slipping into darkness.

It stopped suddenly when someone, something, caught her gently and held her in an embrace similar to a lover's. They, it, was caressing her, shushing her. Part of her let go and listened to the coaxing, while the other fought with everything she was. That part made her open her eyes and she recoiled with a scream that echoed through space.

Death.

A skeleton dressed in a black robe stood -floated- before her. Its hood was up and shrouded its shattered skull in shadows darker than anything imaginable. Mariya swallowed nervously and gathered herself up, showing no fear in her eyes when she stared the figure down.

She hoped.

Mariya's entire body was shaking from fear, making it hard to stand tall. The figure shrieked in rage and fire started to glow in its empty eye sockets. First red, then deep blue. A scythe appeared in its hands, the blade reflecting light although there was no source present. Mariya went to take a step back, but paused when she noticed her reflection in the blade. Transfixed, she looked at the reflection only to see her own death.

Esiviel was kneeling on a blood-stained stone floor, clutching her lifeless form to his chest. Her clothing was stained crimson, a small stream forming a puddle on the floor under them. All kinds of cuts and lacerations covered Esiviel, but she realized he wasn't the one bleeding. Tears ran down his cheeks, and she could only focus on that. Everything else clouded, and she started to feel herself fall into an unseen abyss.

Her eyes started to close and a feeling of peace swept over her. Extreme peace, unbelievable bliss. She welcomed it, embracing the release it brought. It was like the world was melting away and she could finally let go.

'Everything will be fine,' she heard someone say. 'You can rest.'

Part of her did let go, while another didn't. And never would. That part was the one that held onto life tightly, treasuring the gifts of light and happiness: the pain of heartbreak and the joy of warm blood after a nights hunt. She didn't want to forget, yet she didn't want to remember. It was like she was actually hanging from the edge of the light realm and dangling into the darkness, her grip slowly loosening as time passed. Even with the memories of sun and warmth, love and hate, joy and sorrow, and all the human emotions she loved, she had no idea why she was hanging on with so much passion.

Numbly, she looked down at the abyss that reached for her. Once again, she looked up at the blinding light. 'Why?' She heard someone ask, 'Why do you hold on so, Mariya? Let go. All the pain will go away. Cast your bleeding heart into the abyss, release what ails you. Release yourself from your suffering.'

'It's true.' Mariya thought back, her mind finally clearing the fog that had clouded her judgement. 'I do suffer, and I know that I'm finally falling apart at the seams. But there's someone who needs me, even if I only cause suffering to the ones around me. . .He. . .'

Mariya bolted upright in bed, her breathing harsh and labored. She was back home, in her room. Her domain. The dark silk sheets clung to her frame tightly from a cold sweat, showing her sickly form. She had grown to be like this ever since the nightmares started, ever since that one vision rattled her shattered soul into awakening. She rarely ate or fed, and her health started to reflect her self-abuse. Just to prove her thoughts, Mariya held out a hand and smothered a squeak of surprise.

She was shaking so violently. Or course it could have been from the nightmare-ish vision but it seemed too unlikely when she remembered her position. She was sick, she knew it. Her body screamed for blood, food, anything. Mariya felt as if she was the weakest thing alive, more brittle than the youngest baby. Her nightmares only made it worse, foreshadowing and only giving the smallest of hints at answers that she wanted so badly. They were taunting her, reminding her of the frightening reality that was her daily life. The chaos was so much that she had been forgetting to take of herself in the middle of a rescue! Mariya sighed, knowing she was slowly killing herself out of nothing but pure fear.

With a scowl, Mariya hung her head in slight shame just as the door opened. She instantly snapped back to reality and tensed. She also realized she was almost completely stripped, save for her thin tank-top that only served to conceal her breasts. Blushing, she pulled her sheets up around her nervously, almost laughing at her fear. Just as quickly, she let her guard down the slightest bit when a familiar face peeked around the corner.

"How many times do you plan on dying?" Kristopher asked sarcastically. He smiled and invited himself in, half closing the door behind him. "Just so I can tell Anna-Marie how many times she has to drag your soul from the other side." He pulled the chair from her vanity table alongside her bed and sat down. "You need to take better care of yourself, Mariya." His tone changed completely to a more gentle sound, "We could barely bring you back this time, all because your body was in such poor condition."

Mariya nodded, "I know."

It was silent for a moment. Mariya swore her pounding heart was the loudest sound in the room at the time. Her body begging for death, but her inner-self fighting back to claim its stake. That's all there was, confusion.

Pain.

Fear.

After a few moments, Kristopher coughed uncomfortably to catch Mariya's attention. "You need to feed, don't you?"

"If you're volunteering, the answer is no," Mariya muttered in a menacing tone.

Kristopher shrugged, but out of the corner of her

eye, Mariya saw him pull a sliver of silver out of his coat. The metal sparkled brightly, and Mariya looked at him curiously. With a wince, he pulled the blade across his wrist and a river of red gushed to the surface.

"Kristopher!" Mariya shrieked.

Kristopher remained calm, "You have to choose. You, or me."

Mariya knew he was playing with her soft-heartedness. The fact was that she couldn't let someone die in front of her, no matter what. She also knew that if she let him bleed out, he *would* die. She looked away, frustrated and shaking. Everything in her begged to take him up on his offer. For the longest time she resisted, ignoring the longing that grew in her chest each time she inhaled his scent, the anticipating heartbeat.

Mariya yearned for it so badly, the sweet taste of fresh blood. The warmth it brought her, the feeling of bliss. She sat silently for a few moments, loathing herself for having such a knack for getting herself into these positions.

"Fine," she spat and turned back to him.

Kristopher held out his bleeding arm to her, his expression plain and clear. She couldn't tell what he was thinking, or feeling for that matter. But one thing was for sure, he wasn't scared like most would be. Reluctantly, Mariya placed her lips around the cut and gently lapped up the crimson liquid. It was effortless, she didn't have to try. For several minutes she eagerly sipped, savoring the feeling of his blood running down her throat. Abruptly, she pulled back when she felt his pulse weaken.

"I hate you," she whispered, wiping the blood from her lips.

"You're welcome," he smirked when the color gradually returned to Mariya's skin. He looked at the cut he had made to see it was already starting to heal. "What the..?"

"It's something that happens after a vampire drinks from a victim. The cuts or wounds we drink from heal quickly so that we aren't found out. The only exception is the old fashioned bite, but that heals to a bruise," Mariya explained, taking the moment to slip out of bed and into her dress.

Kristopher looked up at her, startled to see her standing next to him. How did she move so fast? Or even move without making any sound? Mariya grinned and flicked her hair over her shoulder, "I know. Cool, right? It's just another one of those interesting mutations of the vampire anatomy that drives doctors batty. No pun intended." She sighed and looked at herself in the mirror, "I used to relish the day I would be of pure blood." As she continued, it almost started to sound like she was envious of her full blood cousins, "I couldn't wait to give my soul to the moon, to kill my human heart once and for all. But then. . ."

"But then?" Kristopher prompted, tilting his head in interest. She was full of so many mysteries that the night would tell only to the chosen few.

Mariya's tone grew bitter and she glared at her reflection in sudden anger, "I grew up and realized what it meant to be cursed. That it wasn't all fun and magic blessings. It was lonely to be a full vampiress and not be able to raise children. But. . ." She stopped, noticing a note that sat on the edge of her vanity.

It was a folded piece of parchment with her name written on it in a flourishing red script. Further investigation showed the red ink to be blood. The nightmare flashed in her head, and for second, she lost herself. She shook her head to clear her thoughts and recognized the package. The way the rose was laid on of top it, the black petals beginning to wilt at the tips, the red tips of its thorns taunting her. It was the letter she had refused to open earlier; her father had resent it. Mariya shakily reached for and slowly unfolded the paper, dreading its message from death:

Mariya, my love,

How many times must I tell you that you and everyone around you will always suffer? You need to remember, my dear, that I'm always watching you and waiting for you. Of course, it's too late for that girl you love so much. If only you had listened.

With much anticipation, your father,
King Devon Gallion

7. The Blood Spread

It took a minute for the letter's grisly message to soak in. Then it clicked. The nightmares she had been having, they were *visions*. He really *was* dwindling down her connections, killing those she loved one by one. *Your family will always suffer...* A sickened feeling quickly rose in her and just as quickly, she shut it down.

"Mariya?" Kristopher noticed her blank gaze, the way she tried to hide that she was shaking. "Are you okay?"

Mariya swallowed the sob in her throat and nodded, "I'll be fine."

"Can I. . ."

"Have you seen Ivy today?" Mariya asked in fake composure, hoping Kristopher wouldn't question her more.

He shook his head sadly and felt the flare in her aura. He knew she wanted so badly to cry, to scream and let out nearly a century of sorrow. It didn't help any that she was losing everything dear to her. Everyone she loved was disappearing, and she knew that Ivy wouldn't make it. She couldn't. At least Esiviel could fight back or hold on, but that gave her little comfort. It seemed like forever ago he was taken, and she started to doubt that he was still in this world.

Despite the pressure, she acted calm and held everything in. Kristopher felt sorry for her, having to act tough for others gain. He knew the perfect word for it: scapegoat. She never complained about her pain, to protect the ones she loved. She was the one that got hurt while others ran and were fine. But she, and everyone she held dear, would suffer because of her. She was the cause of it all.

Mariya calmly searched the house, although she knew her efforts were in vain. She found herself pausing and listening as if to hear Ivy whispering to her stuffed animals, or humming tunelessly out of optimistic dreams that she would never make real. Mariya was silently praying with naive hope to catch a glimpse of crystal blue eyes, or even see a glimmer of beautiful blonde curls, but found nothing. The entire house was empty without Ivy,

100

but Deryk didn't sense the change in the energy. He went about his activities like normal, occasionally answering a phone call from the town hall although he had the day off.

"Deryk," Mariya caught him when he had a spare moment, "Have you seen Ivy today?"

"She was outside in the rose garden last time I saw her," he paused and dried his hands, wet from doing the dishes, on a towel. Then his eyes grew wide in alarm, "Why, you haven't seen her? That's odd, she's usually attached to you at the hip."

Mariya weakly laughed at the joke, trying to calm her racing heart. It was like it was trying to escape the cage of bones that surrounded it and burst. Deryk had just confirmed her worst fears, making her stomach drop like lead. Naively, she looked around the house once more, then went to the courtyard in the backyard garden. It was a small square surrounded by hedges cut perfectly into box shapes around it. A simple white stone bench sat in the center of it, yellowed by the test of time. A statue of a baby angel was nestled under a huge bush, his head buried in his hands in silent sorrow. The roses had grown against a fan shaped lattice that leaned against the house. All of the beauty seemed to laugh at Mariya, the angel's pose only echoing the turmoil in Mariya's heart.

She silently settled on the gray, rose encrusted bench. Her chest ached, and her heart wept, but she shed not a tear.

Something's wrong with me, she thought, *I should be crying.*

All fell silent and still, even Mariya's mind. It was peaceful, for once, to be in the neutral and not have to worry. She felt numb, but didn't pay any attention. For once, she was at ease as if a burden had been removed from her shoulders. Yet, she knew something was wrong, horribly wrong. There had to be. Mariya cared too much to not be upset, but she couldn't bring herself to shed a tear. Instead of a sob leaving her throat, a note clear as a bell filled the air as she sang softly in the voice of a fallen angel:

What once was comfort,
I now run from
The sky turns purple,
the earth glows red beneath my feet
I close my eyes,
And fall into the abyss

Always searching,
I run all my life wanting something
I sing my lungs out,
hoping someone hears my cries

She stopped short in the middle of a stanza. Mariya was silent for moment, trying to think but her mind wouldn't let her. She scowled and focused harder, but still nothing came. She even closed her eyes and focused just on the idea of thought, but her grip on reality was slipping too much. Like every other time this happened, it felt like something from the other side was pulling her.

No! Mariya screamed in her mind, *I have been relying on others too much. It won't happen again.*

Then it felt like a heavy load had been lifted off of her. Instantly, waves of thought and emotions hit her with such a violent force that, for a moment, she couldn't breathe. She was simultaneously both happy and sad, calm and overactive. Then the undertow of grief dragged her under and refused to let her go back to the shore. Her eyes watered heavily, and with a sniffle, she held back the overwhelming sadness with little success.

It all came back to the same thing.

She had to fight her father.

No matter what it meant.

Even death couldn't stop her.

Yet, she needed help and she knew it. With a sigh, Mariya gave herself a few moments to come to terms with Ivy's "death". Drawing in a shuddering breath and wiping the tears from her face, Mariya stood and straightened out her skirt. After a confident nod, she went inside, knowing she was only saying goodbye to the life she loved. Closing the door behind her, she turned to go upstairs and pack, but was stopped short by Deryk.

"What have you done!?" he demanded, his eyes hazed in confused anger. "You killed her!" he looked at Mariya with a sharp stare, accusing her of everything, "You killed my Ivy!"

Mariya kept her face unreadable, passive. "I did no such thing, Deryk," she said flatly.

"It's all because you're here! You're the reason that half the town is dead!" He shouted back, pointing out the already obvious reality before her, making her cringe.

"Deryk, I. . ." Her voice grew weak in her human attempt to reason with him, trying to fight back the frustrated tears that welled to the surface.

"I was wrong to let you in," Deryk regained himself, his voice calm. "I knew that letting a. . .a. . . devil in would only cause trouble," he purposefully mislabeled Mariya, knowing how much it irritated her to call her kind evil. "I gave you a chance, for Ivy's sake, but I pass judgement on you now."

Mariya's face remained impassive, knowing what came next. "You have no right to do that," she whispered lowly, her eyes smoldering heavily with sudden disgust for the human kind. Then a shock hit her, she was thinking like one of pure blood. She now considered herself separate from her human side. With something like a snort of disgust, she turned and practically willed herself to "her" room.

She packed what little she could in her favorite bag,

a messenger's bag made of black canvas-like fabric. She quickly grabbed some of her treasured possessions: a necklace from Esiviel, a "birthday" card from Ivy, her photo album, as well as some of her clothes and the jar of money that sat on her desk. With a sigh, she slung the bag over her shoulder and walked to the door. Mariya only paused for a moment, before flinging it open and stepping in the hall and turning to shut the door before she could have second thoughts.

She went back to the living room and gathered herself up, looking Deryk in the eyes. She let her true nature show, let the swirling colors in her eyes reflect the servant of the moon within her. "You can ban me all you want," she said lowly, her black bangs barely covering her eyes, making her calm facade disappear instantly, "But you *will* regret the day that you said, in front of the gods and all their creation, that Mariya Gallion was evil. You will remember the day the blood rain started."

She went to the front door and opened it slightly, pausing to look over her shoulder. "Because on this day, November 16, in the year of 1916 the queen of the damned was born."

Mariya nervously glanced at the crumpled piece of paper in her hand again. An address had been scribbled on it, and she could barely make out what it said. With a sigh, she walked slowly down the ruined cobblestone road. The rocks were crooked and out of place, making the going rough. She couldn't imagine driving on this in a car. Vines grew up the fragments of brick walls that once separated large, colonial style houses from the street. A few half-rusted gates marked the property lines, but served no other purpose.

Mariya stopped in front of a particularly odd looking mansion. It was built in red brick, following suit of many of the other houses on this street. Vines of ivy grew up the west side of the house, giving it an old world charm. Golden numbers on its crumbling brick fence marked its placement on the street. As if reassuring herself, Mariya nodded and walked up the fractured pathway to the house.

The gardens were filled with all kinds of plants and flowers, many of which Mariya had never seen or heard of. The old mansion was situated on a square piece of land, making the plot of land rather small in relation to some of the others. The roof was covered in old slate shingles, and moss grew in between some of the bricks. Shutters clung for dear life from old hinges that were starting to rust. The windows were tinted, she noticed, and a few even had cobwebs in the corners.

With a sigh, Mariya looked at the antique door knocker and decided to knock normally. She relaxed slightly, tapping the tips of ballet-like shoes on the edge of the slab of cement that was the front porch. After a few moments, she knocked again but there was still no answer.

Are they even home..? She wondered. Carefully, and feeling slightly guilty, she turned the huge, brass doorknob slowly and peaked in. "Kristopher?" She called out.

The house was dimly lit with candles. The door opened into a large main hallway with various rooms on either side before it led to a staircase. It looked like something out of those haunting specials that run at night.

"Hello?" She called again, but only her voice echoing off the walls answered her.

With a look of consternation, Mariya turned and shut the door. With a sigh, she sat for awhile on the steps, waiting to see if they were just out at the moment. She rested her head in her hands, lazily humming to help keep her spirits up. For about fifteen minutes, she sat there. Finally, the door slowly creaked open.

"Can we help you?" Mariya heard a small voice behind her.

"Oh!" Mariya stood up, startled, and turned to face the person. "Yes, I was. . ."

She stopped suddenly, realizing it was Anna-Marie. Like usual, ratty bangs covered her face and eyes, but the main portion of her hair was pulled back into a ponytail.

Anna-Marie stared at Mariya for a moment with owl-like eyes. Ending the silence abruptly, she sighed and called, "Daddy!"

She stepped aside and let Mariya in, but didn't take her eyes off of her. Mariya shivered, it was like she could see into her, reading the secrets in the deepest recesses of her mind. A light breeze blew over them, but neither paid it any mind.

Just like time.

Like life.

Kristopher soon joined the two, his hair in a state of disarray. Still, he managed a warm smile, "Mariya, it's good to see you."

Mariya gave her customary curtsy of gratitude when Kristopher took her bag from her, "Thank you, and it's good to be seen."

"Good. Now, if you please. . ." He looked at Anna-Marie in a way that made Mariya's stomach drop like lead, "We have much to talk about."

The room was stiff, silent. Yet Kristopher and Anna-Marie acted as if it was nothing. The air was saturated, like it was before Devon had possessed her. The air was pure energy, making Mariya restless. She suddenly felt like a caged animal but willed the feeling down. Nothing was going to happen to her. She was safe here.

She hoped.

The chandelier in the room was dimmed, the rainbows of the crystal barely showing in the darkness.

She thought she smelled sage burning, probably to keep at a certain level of psychic activity. Then it shifted and the room flashed like she was going to fall into one of her sudden visions. Then she noticed this was the point of this room, to induce mental activity.

"Mariya," Kristopher started, holding out his hand, "Come here."

Mariya nodded and tentatively took his hand. Kristopher promptly led her to a room that was even worse than the previous one. The air in here choked her it was so thick. She could feel her eyes flash colors the instant she stepped in behind him. The atmosphere was warm yet abrasive, as if it was trying to get into her. She pulled back, trying to wiggle out of Kristopher's grip. Something was unnatural in this room, and it awakened the most animal of instincts inside Mariya.

It always comes back to fear.

"Please. . ." she begged, tugging away.

It was like the back room at the club; a sacred place where the two planes were in perfect harmony. She closed her eyes to clear her mind, but a strong wave of unease and dread enveloped her. Just as quickly, she opened her eyes again. Mariya felt Kristopher let go of her hand, sure she wouldn't run now. Just as he did so, she finally realized a whole wall of the small room was a mirror. At first, an image of herself stared back at her, but only her. She couldn't see the other wall or Kristopher in the image, it was only herself looking back at her with wild eyes. Her black hair was in disarray, mimicking her desperate eyes and sickly frame.

She was almost transfixed, like she was seeing herself for the first time. A few moments later, a new energy filled the room. It was like that of a seance; thick, confused, chaotic, unsettling.

Yet it was still so calming.

Mariya closed her eyes and pictured the energy as Zethin once taught her. A deep purple filled her vision: comforting, regal, supporting.

"Sympathy," Mariya guessed in a low voice, opening her eyes again, slowly this time.

"No," Kristopher softly corrected her. "Memory."

Mariya looked at mirror completely as if she could figure out some unknown secret. Then she blinked and she thought she saw the surface shatter. She closed her eyes and shook her head to clear the vision, then looked at the surface again. It was the same as before, smooth and unbroken. Confused, and a little scared, she looked at Kristopher questioningly.

"You're just fighting the purpose of this room, Mariya." He sighed, "And that isn't a normal mirror. It's like a reverse scrying mirror, in the sense that it doesn't invoke the visions but projects them so that others may see what you, or anyone using it, is seeing."

Mariya quickly spun on her heels to face him

completely, outrage in her eyes. Her eyes were cold, angry and lipping with disgust at the thought. "What?!" She fought back the tears that filled her eyes as they usually did when she was upset, "You expect me to relive those horrid things?!"

"Mariya, in order to help you we have to understand your thought patterns and see what you see," Kristopher tried to keep his voice even, but his impatience started to bleed through.

"So you're treating me like a psycho ward patient?" Mariya dared him, aura flaring. "What if I faint again? What if I don't come out of it this time, or Anna-Marie can't pull me back? You're already know I'm walking, no running, on thin ice as is. I'd rather not push my luck," Mariya growled back, her eyes smoldering.

Kristopher sighed and gently turned her around, making her face the mirror. "I promise nothing will happen, but things will only work out if you did exactly as I say." He felt Mariya tense even more. "Mariya, you have to trust me. We're not here to hurt you. You can let your guard down here, it's your last haven."

Mariya again went to retort, but he cut her off, "Nothing will happen. The second you start to feel pain, you're out. Okay?"

"Promise?" Mariya's tone had changed completely. Her rage had been replaced by childish fear and unease. Her voice was now weak and broken, she would have rather been anywhere but here.

"Promise." He smiled when Mariya's aura died back down as she relaxed. "Good, now I'm gonna walk you through this. Stay with me, don't drift off."

"Huh?" Mariya's pulse climbed again.

"Shh. . .nothing. Just listen to my voice. Don't focus on anything else." He walked in front of her. "Alright, clear your mind of everything. I mean everything, Mariya. No fear, pain, memories, nothing. You're here and now, nothing else matters right now."

Mariya nodded and closed her eyes, taking a deep breath. She felt herself start to slip, but Kristopher called her back. "No wandering, stay with me. Don't go anywhere until I tell you to. Alright?" Mariya nodded, "Good, now if a color comes to your mind let it." Just as he said those words, she flinched when a deep red exploded within her.

A small pain, similar to being pricked with a pin, formed in her palms. Then it intensified, as if someone had stabbed a stake straight through them. Instantly, her breathing grew rapid in response to the ethereal pain. The red then deepened and her view shifted so she was looking over a field.

The grass was a deep crimson, not the usual, gentle green she was used to. Then it shifted again and her heart raced, wondering what was happening. She was looking out into the distance, the sky blotted out by a thick cloud of smoke on the horizon. The sun and the moon both shown over her, and she felt their pull. They were fighting over her heart, who got to rule over her.

'But why are they out at the same time..?' Mariya wondered, trying to ignore both the pain in her hands and the tugging at her chest.

There was a chase between the two, a race of the sorts. The sun would circle as fast as it could; and the moon would follow, only a few inches behind it. It would be a short time before it caught up, then the race would start again, the roles reversed. The light would follow their movements as well, light and then deepest of darkness.

During this time, the fire had spread over the field and now circled her. She couldn't feel the heat or the flames licking at her pale skin, though. It wasn't there.

Neither was her mind.

She was completely gone, her gaze weakly focused on the race in the heavens. Her heart followed it, switching back and forth between her pitiful self and the powerful vampiress that lurked around the corner.

In both her vision and reality, she fell to her knees in sudden pain. Her chest ached and burned, like someone had replaced her heart with fire. In reality, she could hear Kristopher curse to himself as she clutched her head in her hands, ice cold tears streaming down her cheeks. She curled into a tight ball just as another pain exploded in her, her heart feeling like it was going to burst out of her chest. In the vision, the flames engulfed her and threatened to suffocate her.

"Please. . ." she whimpered to no one in particular, wishing the pain would just stop.

She felt someone kneel next to her and put an arm around her shoulders. The contact was agonizing, but she couldn't move to pull away even if she wanted to. She realized the person was muttering something in Latin, and she picked out the last line:

Free her.

Right as he said it, a pressure was released in her and she moaned. Her vision narrowed into a tunnel as her eyelids fluttered shut. With a suddenly heavy exhale, she went limp in Kristopher's arms.

Dead to the world.

8. Hopeless Hearts

"Daddy," Anna-Marie tugged at her brother's sleeve, "Do you like Mariya?" She asked the question so innocently, her eyes twinkling. But that really hit Kristopher; could his sister really believe that he loved Mariya?

He started to retort, but stopped himself. For a moment he thought about it, not sure of the honest answer to that question. Even *he* didn't truly know, which scared him. "Anna. . ." he sighed and picked up his sister, "I'm not sure."

He had put Mariya to bed after her episode, worried. What happened that made her faint? That room was supposed to be perfectly safe, protective. On top of that, it was the first time he had ever seen someone faint from a vision. There was something much bigger here that she wasn't telling them, and Kristopher had a feeling she would never admit. Even more troubling than Mariya's stubbornness or the rarity of the situation was the fact that the mirror had shattered after she fainted. And for a split second before, it had gone pitch black.

Even though she was unconscious, Mariya was still fighting what was happening. Even unconscious, her soul was waging war on some unseen force within herself. It was obvious: the tenseness around her eyes, her slight whimpers, the high concentration of energy around the heart chakra. It was the center of being for all living things, and the main focus point of energy flow through the body. The abundance of energy around that chakra for Mariya meant she was fighting everything. She was resisting her powers, forcing them back down into her in hopes that they would die off and disappear. But they wouldn't. In fact, the resistance only made them all the stronger. The more she fought them, the more her subconscious wanted them. And the circle would only end when she admitted it: she was magic.

There was no other way.

Man is responsible for his own suffering, Kristopher thought with a sigh, putting Anna down and settling on the couch. *If only she could see that and stop this madness. She's so. . .lost. I don't think she has the willpower to save herself, much less her lover. Oh gawd. . .he* sighed in frustration and Anna looked at him questioningly. "Nothing, Anna."

"She can make it through," Anna smiled, sitting down next to her brother. "She only has to see what you and I do."

"It's not going to be that easy, Anna."

"Why, not?" she pouted, her hands on her hips.

"The reason she came so late, from my understanding of what she has told me, is that psychic abilities are looked down upon in her culture. Yes, they tolerate it, but it is considered a gift that they should hide," Kristopher explained, leaning back against the beaten hunk of fabric they called a couch.

"Why?"

He shook his head, "She wouldn't say. Directly anyway."

Anna-Marie got her trademark stubborn look. "Well, she's gonna have to learn to deal with it and stop being such a wimp."

Kristopher shook his head in disbelief at his sister's determination. She never ceased to amaze him. Never. He sighed and looked at the ceiling, his mind working overtime. He knew Mariya had seen something he hadn't and no matter how he questioned her, she would refuse to tell. Her inner self was an enigma, maybe even to Mariya herself, and she wanted to keep it that way. He grinned. Mariya was dark and mysterious, mystic even, just like the many vampire stories he had heard growing up. She had a certain ambience around her that attracted attention without her consent. It was the energy around her, her thought pattern, her proper yet so childish way of acting that made others wonder just who she really was. And Kristopher intended to find out.

Mariya awoke several hours later, exhausted. She couldn't feel any of her limbs, it was as if someone had dipped her in some kind of numbing cream. She laid awake in the afternoon light, but didn't dare open her eyes. For a second, she found peace in the calm abyss that greeted her in the recesses of her mind. With a sigh, Mariya let her eyes lazily open and look up at the slight veil that covered the four-post bed. A thin piece of black, chiffon-like fabric hung from the top of the bed and cascaded down the rest of it, concealing her from the rest of the world. It was like looking through a fog, the world outside of her protective veil was only a blur. Silently, she wished it was and that it was all just a horrid dream that she was still alive. All for one reason:

If she wasn't dead, she would go through another painful vision.

With a moan, Mariya sat up and smoothed down her bedraggled hair. With a sigh, she went to part the curtain of black to get up, but hesitated. She knew, or at least had a feeling, that Kristopher would question her about what happened to make her black out.

And to make the mirror shatter.

Mariya shook the notion off quickly, maybe he wouldn't. Maybe, miraculously, he would let it slip. *Right, and vampires are really sensitive to garlic and holy water. But seriously, if it had made me faint the first time, why make me relive it?* Regretfully, she dragged herself out of bed and realized she was only in her full length slip. With a blush of recognition, she quickly slipped her dress on.

As she left the room, she caught sight of her reflection in the full length mirror on the opposite wall. She took several steps backwards and looked at herself after pulling back the heavy curtains to let some light in. Mariya titled her head in thought, noticing that her eyes were a shade darker, her skin paler.

Is it my time? She questioned, staring back hard at her reflection. *I've been of half blood for awhile. . .so maybe No. Not yet.* She dismissed the idea from her mind almost instantly. *She hasn't come to claim me, she knows I have something more to do before I can serve her and my kind.*

With an exasperated sigh, Mariya made her way down the hall. The wood floor was cold under her feet, making her want to hurry. Part of her mind wandered back to the night when her mother was killed, but she pushed the images away almost instantly. Mariya calmed herself down, taking deep breaths and ignoring the tugging in her chest.

119

Regardless of fear, she took her time, and humming tunelessly, her mind began wandering again. Then reality came crashing down on her when she walked down the stairs and into the living room. Kristopher was reading, relaxing in the only arm chair in the sparsely decorated room. A small smile crossed his face when her heard the skin of Mariya's naked feet lightly tapping on the wooden floor, but his eyes said something totally different when he looked up at her.

Sweet moon, Mariya thought to herself, a sinking feeling rising inside her, *what does he want from me?*

"Cut to the chase," she snapped, surprising both Kristopher and herself with the uncharacteristic anger in her voice.

Kristopher calmly sighed and flipped his book shut after gently folding the corner of a page over. "Anna-Marie and I talked about your recent happening, and we've decided to put your training at a slightly slower pace." He paused to let her think about it, then continued when he saw the confusion in her eyes. "So you don't hurt yourself."

"Meaning?" Mariya prompted, her voice unsure.

Kristopher sighed again, "We're putting it on hold for a little while so you can get your bearings."

Mariya shrugged, her calm composure betraying the devastated pain in her. "Fine. You two are in charge." *I'm so sorry, my love,* she thought to herself, *but it will have to*

take a little while longer. *I'm sorry if I've already failed you.*
She finished, going to "her" room and blinking back the
ashamed tears that burned in her eyes.

Mariya tried her best to stay upbeat, distracting
herself with meaningless chores around the shop and
house. It was mind numbing, and Mariya's blood started
to boil again. She was restless, her mind always reaching
out of her frail body and trying to find Esiviel's energy.
Every time, though, she found nothing. Over time, she
stopped trying and hope eventually started to dwindle for
her. She started to sneak out at night like she used to
when she was princess, to run under the stars and feel the
chill of the night air on her skin. But just like she was a
child again, Kristopher would drag her back home.
Eventually, she even gave that up and started something
she never thought she would.

Life got boring, and only the pain she brought
herself every night told her she was still alive. Her wrists
were now almost a solid line of red; the ugly, red lines she
had carved in herself laughing at her every time her
sleeve would slip or she would cut again. As far as she was
concerned, hope was gone and there was no point in
fighting if everything she loved had already been ripped
away from her. Like before, Mariya refused eating, both
the human and vampire kind, and grew sickly. Kristopher
had to force her several times to at least feed, just out of

the hope she wouldn't completely give up on life.

But she had.

Mariya would sometimes wonder if she would stay like this, and sometimes she thought that was okay. This state of mind worried her keepers, while the townspeople were pleased. They thought the "beast" was tamed, that the two tamed the "monster" that was behind all the heinous murders was gone. And Mariya seemed to agree. If she never went outside or cared, she wouldn't get close to anyone, therefore there was no one her father could kill to hurt her. And then no one suffered.

But Anna-Marie and Kristopher knew different.

Mariya had put *herself* in this state, reassuring herself it was for the best. *No one will get hurt this way, no one will be killed.* If she died, everything would be fine. If she agreed with the townspeople that she was the murderer, she would be left alone. And most of time, she left everything at that, the same haunting thought echoing through her night after horrifyingly long night:

It is my fault Ivy's dead, that Esiviel is suffering. It's my fault this ever happened. I ran when my kingdom needed me most, so my father took over. Then look what happened. It's all my fault. Everything. The pain, the suffering, the blood, the tears. Everything.

Of course they tried to coax her out of it, reminding her what she was fighting for. But Mariya would only look at them with a blank stare and, with a shrug, go back to what she had been doing.

Nothing matters anymore. It's over. He won. He got what he wanted. I'm dead, and he can keep the kingdom all he wants. I'll never have to show my face to Council and be crowned. Everything will go according to fate's plan. He won.

Time crawled by, and things only got worse; the cutting, her slipping, the nightmares, everything. Kristopher would watch her with sympathy in his eyes, *She's killing herself with a heavy guilt that isn't hers to bear. It wasn't her fault.*

That night, Mariya was watching the stars as usual. They seemed to calm to her, soothe her unspoken pain. But even then, Mariya pushed it away. Everything slipped through her fingers, and she didn't mind. She watched the twinkling numbly, feeling almost as if she were drunk. Then she laughed.

Her fingers ached to grip it.

They burned, her wrist tingled.

With a sigh, Mariya got up and walked over to her night stand. She looked around, as if someone was watching her every move, then knelt and opened the bottom drawer. Her fingers fumbled as she carefully pulled back the contents of the drawer to reveal a small wooden box. After looking around her room one more time, she lifted it out of the drawer. Sitting cross-legged, Mariya anxiously opened the lid of the box.

Her heart immediately raced at the silver glow. Her eye gained a new twinkle that only love used to bring. Sitting in a small bed of fabric scraps, as if she was protecting it, was a razor blade.

The edge shone brilliantly, sometimes stained with the occasional pink splotch. Her wrists ached longingly at the sight of the metal, and she smiled drunkenly. She cautiously picked the blade up, and set the box on the night stand. Still smiling, she went to her bed and sat on the edge, eyeing the edge of the blade.

Something in her told her not to do it. She could fight it. Something screamed at her this wasn't the answer, that there was another way. She ignored it, placing the blade against her skin and pushing down. Wincing, she slashed.

Pain.

Release.

Red instantly flowed to the surface, coupled by a sharp pain. Mariya stared numbly at the crimson river that snaked its way down her arm. The release was what she sought, the numbness that followed each slash. She had heard somewhere that it was the endorphins, how hurting herself made her happy she still hadn't figured out, that she was addicted to. The rush each cut brought.

Biting her lip, she ran the blade over her skin again and again until she couldn't feel the cuts at all. Then her sanity kicked in.

As usual, she threw the blade aside as her heart raced and adrenaline snaked through her system. Biting her lip and cursing to herself, she reached for her first aid kit. Ignoring the new, piercing pain, she pressed a square of gauze to her wrist, worrying when it bled straight through the thin fabric. Cursing again, she grabbed yet another piece of gauze and added it to the one she already clutched tightly.

Panic flooded Mariya's mind: she had never meant to kill herself. But she couldn't get the bleeding to stop, no matter how long she waited or many squares were added to her makeshift bandage. Biting her lip, Mariya weighed her options.

Things would be better if she let go, she decided. No one would have to worry about who killed who, and her father could rule in her place. It solved everything: the pain, the tears, the fear. Mariya wouldn't have to worry, she could just let go and fall into the abyss that waited with great appetence for her surrender. Then her mind scattered in a million different directions when everything started to slip.

The world narrowed into a tiny speck, and she started to feel light headed. Mariya tried calling for help, but her words turned into a blurred jumble. Her eyes wanted to flitter shut, but she forced her will on just staying awake and trying to stay alert. Everything slipped more, and a deep, throaty laughter reached her ears. She felt herself numbly fall onto her side against the soft blankets of her bed.

Then she felt it.

A complete release hit her, a total numbness to everything else. A high keening sounded somewhere far off, Mariya pushed it away for the beautiful light that surrounded her. She was weightless, floating and in complete bliss. There were heavy footsteps, but she ignored it. They were so heavy, too loud for her. She wanted the light.

The comfort.

"Mariya!" She heard someone call far off.

His voice is nice, soft. Why is he here? Who is he?

"Mariya," the boy shook her shoulders, "C'mon, sweetie, stay with us."

But the light. . .it's so comforting. . .Why would I..?

"Don't you-?"

Then he noticed the slashes on her wrists and the pool of blood that made the dark comforter glint wetly. Mariya still held the gauze to her wrists weakly, but it had soaked all the way through. Every sheet was now a dark crimson and grew darker with each pump of her heart.

"Oh my. . ." he looked at Mariya with sympathy in his eyes, "Why didn't you tell me..?"

The light reached out and brushed Mariya lightly, trying to pull her into it. She fought it back, though, transfixed with the scene of her own death before her. It was like she was watching it through a cloud, it seemed far off and dream-like. Yet, she felt it when Kristopher pulled the gauze off her wrists. She winched and looked at her wrists, surprised to see a red band across them.

Wasting no time, Kristopher quickly stopped the bleeding. Mariya winced when an invisible force tried to pull her back as he muttered a simple spell. She fought it, resisting with all her strength. She didn't want to go back to the pain, she wanted peace. This was what she wanted, not to go back to the pitiful existence she had just left.

The light.

Then she was completely gone, and everything went black. She felt steady, but it wasn't the end. It was far from over. Heaven, or Hell, wasn't like this. It couldn't be. There was too much pain for her to be dead. Then the keening came back.

Endless screams.

Gone.

9. Moonlight Magic

Then it all changed one day. Mariya was sweeping near the "mirror room", when something woke up in her. She felt as if she had been slapped in the face first thing in the morning. Blinking, she leaned the broom against a wall and looked around. No one was watching, so she cautiously peeked into the room. Sensing nothing wrong, Mariya shrugged and stepped into the room, catching sight of herself in the mirror.

Pain.

Awakening.

Fear.

She saw herself lying in a bloody pile, a circle of flames around her motionless corpse. Her pale face was frozen in an expression of inexplicable horror, her now forest green eyes locked on herself.

In reality, Mariya suddenly fell to her knees, her chest aching. It felt as if someone had stabbed her from behind, then twisted the blade and pulled it back out with an angry flourish. As if it had really happened, she coughed up blood, clutching her aching sides. Her fingers tightly curled into fists against the fabric of her dress, her overly sharp nails faintly digging into her skin. Mariya felt like she was burning, but from the inside out, as if someone had replaced her blood with liquid fire.

She collapsed, coughing even harder although her aching body begged her not to. A puddle of thick, clot-like blood formed from her coughing; and just as quickly Kristopher was at her side, shushing her. Something like a whimper passed her lips before she broke into another coughing fit, bringing up more blood.

"Mariya. . ." Kristopher whispered soothingly, "You have to relax. I can't help you when you're fighting it so badly. C'mon sweetheart. . ."

But his voice trailed off in an annoying buzz to Mariya. A red haze filled her eyes as the flames danced around her, licking at her skin but never leaving a mark. Suddenly, the flames disappeared and Mariya was on the ground on all fours in a dark room with her father standing before her, a wicked grin on his face.

"Mariya, my love, how nice of you to join us," his

welcoming voice betrayed his twisted expression.

Us? Does he have something to do with this?

"It's a pity, though, really. You were a little too late to say goodbye to your wretched mate. I must say, though, he was a fine cut of meat."

"*What?!*" Mariya nearly screamed, her eyes flying to her father's face.

"Yes, he was a rather fine find, better than some of those worthless humans, although the wine left much to be desired." He sighed in mock sadness, "Probably a bad year. Pity really."

Don't listen to him, Mariya, she coached herself, just as another fit of coughing hit. *He's only taunting you. He didn't die like that. . .he couldn't have.*

"Ah, but he was only the appetizer. You, my dear, are the main course."

Esiviel grinned, feeling Mariya's frightened determination seep through their bond. He hated that he had to cause her pain to pull her back to reality, but it was good to have the old Mariya back. Unfortunately, that stunt had robbed him of most of the energy left in him. Now, he was just barely hanging on.

Rip!

He drew in a gasp of pain as the sound of metal meeting brick rang in his ears. Like usual, a sharp pain followed the sound, dulled by his loss of blood. A blade was, once again, shoved straight through his chest into the wall behind him. It was only a dull sting to him, a far off pain.

"She'll come," came a seductive voice in his ear.

Esiviel's eyes started to flitter shut, the only shred of consciousness he had left slipping through his fingers. "No, no she won't. . ." he dozily whispered back.

At least, that's what he hoped, and prayed for with all of his existence. Because if she did come, death waited.

And it wouldn't take 'no' for an answer.

Training for Mariya quickly picked up, more intense than before and just as relentless. She was always in pain, but ice packs and deep tissue messages kept her going. All the while she pushed through it, although the back of her mind begged her to stop. Something, a small part of what little sanity she had left, yelled at her to stop this self-mutilation.

But she always ignored it. She had to, this wasn't about just her anymore. Mariya had an obligation to fulfill, and nothing could stop her. No matter what the price seemed to be and how she was broken.

She winced, just learning how to control the fire she summoned. It burned at her, threatening to take her hand with it. Biting her lip, Mariya simply summoned a small barrier around her hand to keep the flames at bay.

"Good," Kristopher praised, nodding. "Now, shape

it. Let it become part of you and show what you are."

"What?!"

As soon as Mariya lost attention, they burned into her again. Hastily, she put the barrier back up. She looked at her hand cautiously, tilting it in various direction as if she was transfixed by her own magic. Relaxing, she let the shield down but to her amazement, the flames didn't burn. They seemed to just gently caress her skin, brushing it gently as if to reassure her. Completely relaxing, Mariya cupped her hands in front of her. She watched in amazement as the two smaller flames combined into one. Blinking, she looked at Kristopher for an explanation.

"You willed it to be that way," he shrugged, walking over to stand next to her. "Now, as I said, completely let go of control."

"But they'll. . ." She didn't look away from the small blaze, but her voice was hesitant.

"Mariya," he sighed impatiently, "They won't burn you, trust me. They won't. . .not where they're coming from."

"What do you mean. . .?"

"Nothing," he shook his head in dismissal. "You have to trust yourself here. Now come on, let go."

The second she did, the flames turned into a huge blaze, flaring into one tall flame. Mariya squeaked in surprise, but managed to keep control of it. The flames danced rapidly, flickering as if a breeze was blowing over them. For a split second, they turned a deep navy color before going back to a reddish orange.

But my energy is purple. . .Mariya blinked and looked at Kristopher, completely dismissing the flames and shaking her hands until only a thin smoke rose from them. "Explain what's really going on," she nearly growled.

"Moving on," Kristopher sighed and just launched her into another task.

This went on for days, and all the while Mariya never forgot the split second those flames were that odd color. Was it possible that she was able to "borrow" another's energy without her knowing? No. That took years to master, she couldn't have. Yet, it did seem logical. She was the One, so maybe it could have been from that. With a groan, Mariya flopped on her bed and stared at the ceiling.

The white paint was so smooth, so calm as compared to what she was going through. Although her muscles screamed no to, she reached up to the ceiling with her fingers outstretched. *So what caused it? I know Kristopher is represented by the color blue, but Anna.* . .*no. She uses fire, but she wasn't in the room. How could she have helped? Why would she have helped? She hates me. Maybe, just maybe, it was.* . .She twirled her finger around playing with the dust particles that were visible in the last rays of sun that peered through her blinds. *No,* she shook her head, *he's probably in no shape to help me right now seeing as where he's standing is a lot worse. But still, blue is his color.* . .She curled

134

her hand into a fist suddenly, and the dust rushed away from her in a hurried panic.

Sighing, she rolled over on her side and curled into a tight ball. *Kristopher's hiding something. But what?* "It's not like he has anything to hide from me," she mumbled, finishing her thoughts out loud. "Oh well, I'll get it out of him. . ." her eyes started to flitter shut, the word narrowing down into a small tunnel. "Eventually. . ."

Sighing peacefully, she let her eyes close her mind wonder. In the corner of the consciousness, she felt someone rub her back soothingly but she was too far gone. *I love you. . .* was Mariya's last thought before the night descended on her and refused to let go.

The peace didn't last long, as she was at it again right after breakfast. This time, though, she was the one who did the eager prodding for that day's session. She spent all morning reviewing previous lessons and learning new exercises as well: lighting a candle from across the room, making the lights in a room turn on and off at will, accessing her energy quicker and quicker, and then came the true test.

It was a sort of a graduation. Mariya had attempted this exercise before, but today was the final chance she had to figure it out. It seemed simple enough: she had to light the room with her energy. Nothing but her aura. With a sigh, she settled on the small stool in the middle of the room, waiting for Kristopher's signal.

"Alright, Mariya," Kristopher sighed, "We're going to try this again."

Mariya timidly nodded, bitting her lip. Kristopher smiled, "You'll get the hang of it, don't worry. Hell, you've already made extremely impressive progress, seeing as your at an intermediate level in less than two weeks."

"Remember I'm naturally psychic," Mariya gently reminded him with a proud smile.

"I know," he ruffled her hair, "Now come on, let's finish this thing. Okay?"

Mariya nodded and closed her eyes gently, folding her hands in her lap. Almost completely blocking out the room around her, she faintly heard the *click* of Kristopher turning the lights off. She unconsciously started to control her breathing, in through her nose and out through her mouth. When she was completely grounded, and she had control over her giddy heartbeat, she let herself subconsciously fall backwards into herself.

Black.

Darkness.

Home.

Taking a deep breath, she pushed even farther into her shattered consciousness. Mariya felt her grip on the material world starting to slip, warning her of the ever slimming time limit she was working with. Ignoring it, she pushed further to find the ever fading ball of energy hidden deep within her. In reality, she gave a pained grimace and pushed herself beyond the barrier that she had made to protect herself. Almost instantly, she was through into a vast abyss filled with pain and suffering. Part of her tried to pull herself out of the agonizing energy, while the other fought to hold on.

A moan escaped her lips just as she fully let herself slip. After a soft exhale and a slightly loader moan, the room was filled with a blinding wave of dark purple energy that almost took on the form of a creeping mist. Mariya took in a labored breath then forced herself to let go and wake up, her eyes shooting open.

After relaxing for what only seemed like a second and taking no time at all to catch her breath, Mariya looked at Kristopher hopefully. With a smile, he nodded solemnly. A sparkle of hope returned to Mariya's eyes, a smile spreading across her lips.

"Thank you," Mariya muttered as they walked to the living room. She was dizzy and a bit lightheaded so Kristopher served as her crutch, letting her put an arm around his shoulders.

"For what?" He looked at her questioningly, helping her sit on the couch.

"For not giving up," she murmured lightly, her lips barely moving. "And as sappy as it sounds," she looked up at him and smiled, "for helping to find me when even I couldn't."

"You have someone else to thank as well," Kristopher smiled, leaning back and looking at the ceiling.

"He's been watching over you, Mariya," he explained, seeing her want to interject. "Even though *he's* the one that needs the help, he worries about you. In fact, I believe he watches over you in your sleep, just as he always would."

Mariya nodded understandingly, tightly clutching the necklace Esiviel had given her when he came back from his annual trip across Europe: a small, silver crescent moon with a star delicately balanced on the bottom point. "Who?" she asked, although she already knew who it was.

"A young man, only slightly older than you," he started thoughtfully, "I can feel his love from your bond. In fact, he's with you right now. . .if you know what I mean."

Mariya choked back her tears of relief, but a tear managed to silently rolled down her near porcelain colored cheek. "He's still alive. . ." she muttered, shaking her head in disbelief. "After all this time, he's still here. I can't believe that idiot. . ." her voice trailed off into a light sob.

"Mariya?"

"How can you tell he's "with" me?" she asked quietly, looking at the ground.

"I just feel someone's energy following you. It's protective, loving, fierce, yet so gentle. I just know it has to be. . ." Kristopher cut himself off, noticing the wet spots that now stained the old carpet. He sighed and comfortingly put an arm around Mariya's shoulders,

"You'll save him, Mariya," he whispered, although his voice sounded tense, unnerved, "You promised him, promised all your kind. Don't worry."

"Thank you," Mariya answered plainly between sobs, burying her face in Kristopher's shoulder, "Thank you for everything."

Mariya eventually cried herself to sleep, but awoke not even an hour later, ready for what lay ahead. So, testing her new found confidence, Kristopher put her through various sparing drills. For a few days he put her through various tests, no matter what the weather.

"But. . .my father's a full. . .he wouldn't fight outside. . ." Mariya timidly objected.

"There's still night," Kristopher countered with a grin, "plus, if you notice, the rain makes you slower on your feet, right?" Mariya nodded, and he continued, "Imagine if you were you used to the resistance. Then, what happens if it all disappeared and you were able to move freely?"

"I'd be able to move faster because I was used to restrictions?" Mariya guessed, looking at him oddly after brushing the rain soaked bangs out of her eyes.

"Exactly. That, *and* you told me Devon was psychically inclined like you, right?" Once again, Mariya nodded and waited for him to continue, "Did you notice that energy work only affects people who are sensitive to it?"

She nodded again, looking confused, as she ran a hand across her face to brush away some of the rain dripping from her bangs. "Yeah, but what does that. . .?"

Kristopher held up an index finger, signaling for her to be patient and let him explain. "Don't you think he would use that against you? He could make the air in the room heavy, or make it seem distorted in some way. What I'm teaching you is not fighting, but how to adapt to your surroundings. I'm teaching you how to use the environment to your advantage, even if it is tough. Understand? *That's* why I make you fight in all kinds of weather."

"You little son of a-!" Mariya started, faking being mad.

"Now, now," Kristopher teased, trying not to look too pleased with himself. "That kind of language wouldn't be appropriate for a young queen, now would it?"

"Yeah I'll show you appro-!" She cut herself off, freezing, "Wait. How did you know I was supposed to be queen?!" She turned quickly to face him, their eyes meeting for the first time since she nearly killed herself during her depression spell, "I haven't told anyone!" Her aura flared and Kristopher winced, knowing he had hit sensitive territory.

He ruffled her hair playfully, "That's one secret I could find out on my own."

"Yeah. . .but how..?" She mumbled, all steam from her previous aggravation completely gone. "That's the

140

one secret I guard with my life. . .I mean. . ."

"I know things about you that I doubt even Esiviel, or *yourself* for that matter, know."

"Like?"

"Your true element isn't fire," he said plainly, then refused to say anymore for the rest of the night.

10. Soul On Fire

The sky was on fire the next night, the oranges and reds from the sinking sun setting the sky ablaze in a display of natural fireworks. Mariya silently watched it all happen, her nervously pounding heart making the blood rush in her ears. Tonight was it.

Her entire existence, her whole being, knew it.

Tonight was the fight with destiny.

Everything was silent, the world frozen in the calm before the storm. The entire universe seemed to be waiting in tense anticipation for the duel that was soon to pass, making Mariya's insides twist with fear.

What if I fail?

What will happen to my kind?

What will happen to. . .to Esiviel?

143

Her mind was racing, her heart keeping pace with it. Everything in her was a giant blur: each breath fading into the other; each heartbeat becoming one long, painfully slow pulse; each thought chaotically flying in and out of her mind at their leisure. Her entire spirit screamed to run, to leave and never, *ever*, come back. To just run, and never give a second thought or look back.

To be free.

But she couldn't do that.

Mariya couldn't run away from what she had been fighting for, the one she loved, or the chance to put the one behind these heinous acts to death. Too much was at stake here, Mariya's breath came heavier as that thought sunk into her.

This is the moment that decides the fate of every living thing.

The moment that decides my legacy.

The beginning of the end for my tale.

She didn't want to fight, she finally admitted to herself as her gaze became focused on the horizon. Mariya couldn't stand the thought of fighting her own flesh and blood, but the ache that hit her heart every time she thought of the innocent victims made her. With a sigh, she closed her eyes but for a moment and saw a wave of red.

The bloody chain of fates leading to her destroyed heart.

"Mariya," Kristopher sighed and sat next to her on

the ledge of the bay window she was perched in. "You don't have to do this."

Mariya mutely nodded to acknowledge he was there. She couldn't link any of her racing thoughts together to form a sentence, much less try to listen to him. With a sigh, she realized it felt like her blood was burning and that each breath became harder than the last.

The time had almost come.

"Mariya. . ." Kristopher started in a cautious voice, taking her hand in his. "Did you hear me?"

That cleared some of the fog in her mind, there was a connection to the physical plane now; she could stay grounded and focus on not going astral. "Yes. . ." she muttered in a weak voice, looking at him. "But I *do* have to do this. Right now, my life means so much more than myself. So many lives depend on me: you, Esiviel, my entire clan, and all of the humans and/or vampires I may never meet. The *world* relies on me tonight, Kristopher."

"Mariya, breathe," he said plainly, feeling her grip in the physical world starting to slip. "Stay grounded and centered. Stay here with me."

Mariya nodded and closed her eyes, consciously willing her breathing to slow and grow deeper. Almost instantly, she felt calmer. Taking one more deep breath, she opened her eyes again and looked at Kristopher. "And I just don't know if I can do it," she picked up again almost instantly, her breathing already growing irregular again.

"Breathe, Mariya."

"But I-!"

"Mariya, calm down." He sighed and let go of her hand, only to have her take his. She *needed* some connection to the plane of living, to feel someone else's energy. Kristopher looked at her in surprise, "What are you..?"

"Please," she begged, her voice pained. "I just need someone near me right now, anyone." He nodded understandingly as she continued. "What happens if I fail and the vampire kingdom, no the entire *empire*, falls because of me? I could never forgive myself," she looked away shamefully.

"But you would be dead," Kristopher pointed out calmly.

"No," Mariya shook her head in disagreement, "I would come back as a full and have to live with my shame."

"Why?"

"If I never claim the throne, my father would rule and he would ruin everything this race has worked for."

"What do you mean "claim the throne"?"

Mariya sighed, "I'm queen by blood, Devon's family is that of the royals. However, I have to be of full blood before I can actually step forward to claim my power as rightful queen." Her heart rate picked up again, and a worried blush lit her pale face.

"Breathe," Kristopher encouraged in a soothing tone

of voice.

"I am," she half-snapped, but was grateful for his concern. "Sorry, I'm just a little. . ."

"Tense, I know." He smiled gently, "I can feel it."

"But really, what if I can't do it?" Mariya asked again, letting go of his hand.

"You'll do fine."

She uncertainly smiled back, "I hope you're right. For everyone's sake."

Then her breath caught.

Her heart skipped a beat.

Something grabbed her from the other side, and wouldn't let go. She winced, (or was it a pitiful, helpless whimper?), at the pain of it all. An unseen hand pulled, yanked, at her heart and refused to let go. Her throat closed up, choking on the suddenly heavy air around her. For a second, she thought she had been pulled into a totally different world, a different place. A different plane.

Mariya fought the contact for awhile, realizing the agonizing sensations were only in her mind. Even with her iron will, her grip slipped and she was thrown into the altered state of being. She felt herself falling, leaving behind the tattered two-story townhouse she had taken up residence in for the past couple of weeks. Then the darkness grabbed hold of Mariya and pulled her into an entirely different place. Naively, she wished it were just another vision and Kristopher would soon pull her out of it.

It all comes back to fear.

Mariya didn't have to open her eyes to know this place was a source of death, the manifestation of Hell on Earth. The air was thick with it, the smell of rotting corpses and age-old blood painting the unseen picture on the back of her eyelids. With a wince, Mariya forced herself to sit up and open her eyes. Just as she feared, the room was completely darkened, save for the blinding overhead lamp that bathed her in a chilling feeling of dread.

She shook her head, hoping to wake up in her bed at Kristopher's house as if it were only a vision. But it wasn't, it didn't clear. It was all real, solid, existing as any other thing would be. She sighed, and after stumbling multiple times from dizziness, got to her feet. She blinked, looking out beyond the safety of the white light that surrounded her. Yet, her night vision failed her and left her purblind.

Then there was a moan from somewhere far off in the darkness.

Or at least it seemed like it. Mariya knew it wasn't her, she would have felt that embarrassing vibration in her chest and throat. Her entire body tensed, and she looked around uselessly. Still, her vision refused to respond to her orders.

"Who's there?" she called, hating the weakness that seeped into her voice.

Only silence met her calls. Nervously, Mariya balled her hands into fists so tight that her knuckles turned white. She was vaguely aware of the fact that she was shaking, but ignored it when she took a step forward into the shadows. Her vision faded in, as if something in the recesses of her mind had found the dimmer switch.

Mariya gasped, recoiling.

Several mutilated corpses were scattered about the room, making the medium sized room look like an abandoned morgue. They were the missing young women from the village, all lying in their eternal resting place. Their throats were all slit, but Mariya knew that wasn't the cause of their death. On each one's neck, almost in the same place on every body, were two small puncture wounds that had started to turn to misshapen bruises.

She thought she had grown used to things like this: the stench of death; the energy of a forced graveyard; the sense of dread that overwhelmed her as she stood in the semi-lit room surrounded by nothing but misery. But she wasn't.

Death always took her by surprise.

She had a human's heart.

Mariya's stomach twisted as she stepped forward yet again. *How could someone, even my father, do this?* She sighed and walked along the walls of the building slowly, saying silent apologies to each and every body in atonement. *Does he want me dead that badly?*

Her eyes teared guiltily as she walked beside the

grisly piles of rotting corpses, noticing how some were further in the process of decomposition than others. Then she paused at the body of a young girl, her blonde hair plastered against her fair skin by blood. She wore a navy blue dress that was torn in places and stained with splotches of crimson. Her face was peaceful, almost like she was sleeping and looked out of place compared to the faces that were frozen in expressions of pure fear. Mariya choked all over again.

Ivy.

There was the sudden rattle of chains, followed closely by the echo of a rough cough. Mariya quickly spun on her heels, braced and ready to fight. Adrenaline snaked through her veins, making her heart race. As soon as the tension was built up, it was gone. Her eyes stung with tears all over again, and she half-hopefully took a step forward.

"Esiviel?" her voice cracked, disbelief seeping into her words.

He weakly looked up at her, silver eyes hazed and distant. With a deeply saddened expression, he shook his head as if willing away a vision. "Go away. . ."

Mariya nervously bit her lip and walked over, kneeling in front of him. "Esiviel, it's really me. No visions, nightmares, illusions, nothing. I promise." She tried to smile, ignoring the tear that ran down her cheek.

Her heart ached looking at him, seeing the condition he was in. One eye was black and swollen shut,

150

while the other was swollen but still open. A trail of blood ran down the side of his face from his right temple and upon closer inspection, Mariya found a huge, open sore from repeated blows to it.

Devon, she growled to herself. Feebly fighting back the tears that now pooled in her hazel eyes, she continued to look Esiviel over.

His entire body was covered in gashes and open sores that had tried to close numerous times, but were reopened just as many times. Worst of all were his wrists, chafed from previous attempts at freedom. Bound by a thick chain, and then looped around an unused pipe, it was a wonder they weren't broken from his resistance.

"Oh. . .my love. . ." Mariya gently brushed his blood crusted hand with hers, "I'm so sorry it took so long. . ."

"Run," Esiviel whispered hoarsely, shoving her apology aside. "Please, Mariya, I beg of you."

"What are you..? Why?" Her heartbeat picked up, her voice unsure.

"*He* brought you here," he answered plainly, looking up at her with pleading eyes. "This is the final act, Mariya. He thinks it's curtain call for you, that it's over."

"Esiviel. . ."

"Just leave. Forget about me. Return to the kingdom and live in safety until your time comes. You'll be safer there; you'll be protected."

"No," Mariya shook her head and looked at her mate, fiery determination lighting her eyes. "We've both come too far for this to be the end. It's not over for us, I've worked too hard for this."

"Mariya, please," Esiviel looked at her with complete honesty. "He brought you here to kill you, and he's not taking no for an answer."

"I don't care!" Mariya snapped, her aura flaring.

"Look-!"

Esiviel was cut off by a melancholy applause that echoed through the small chamber. Mariya sighed, tensing with an inhale. A strong feeling of dread and death washed over her, wanting to pull her under. Mariya pushed it aside and stood, slowly turning on her heels to face the visitor, her determined expression betraying the fear inside her.

"Devon," she addressed him simply, her voice flat with disgust and annoyance.

"Mariya, my dear!" He smiled broadly, as if he was welcoming to her to a five-star casino in Las Vegas. "I'm glad you could make it! It would be such a shame if the star of the ending scene wasn't here for her best, and final, performance."

Mariya remained silent, although her gaze dripped icicles. "Oh, I'm sorry, I've forgotten my manners." He bowed to her and grinned, although his eyes mocked her, "Your highness."

"I'm only here for Esiviel," Mariya ignored his gestures and threats.

"After that touching performance? It would be a

shame for you to not give an encore to it. I'm sure your wretched lover wouldn't mind if I played a small role in it, would he?"

Mariya tensed and braced herself, recognizing the bloodlust in her father's eyes. He continued, "Honestly, my dear, wouldn't you like to stay and enjoy my. . ." A wall of orange and red flared, making a circle around her. "Hospitality?"

The visions that she had endured all this time awakened, but Mariya forced them back. It all made sense now, all the pieces were in place. Then the images came back.

Death.

Choking.

Screaming.

Endless pain.

No, she thought, pushing it all even farther back into her mind and focusing on the task at hand. *It's all an illusion*, she coached herself, realizing the flames didn't burn her. Mariya closed her eyes, *Stay focused. Stay grounded in this plane.* She took in a single breath and the flames almost instantly died down.

Mariya opened her eyes again and stumbled, dizzy from the excess effort. Before she got her bearings back, there was a sharp pain in her back. Gasping, she tried not to tense; the contraction of her muscles would only drive the blade in farther.

"What's wrong, my dear? Not enjoying my

company?" Devon whispered in her ear, twisting the blade and making Mariya cough up a mouthful of blood. "It's a shame really, I had so much planned for you." Swiftly, he pulled the blade out with a flourish, pushing Mariya forward.

With a slight whimper, she fell and caught herself on her hands. Just when the pain from scratching her palms on the rough stone floor caught up, she was kicked in the stomach. Mariya went with the motion of the kick, not resisting when she was sent flying several feet across the room. She laid limply where she landed, hurting everywhere.

She coughed again weakly, blood splattering onto the floor to join the pool already forming beneath her. "Why Devon? What's the point of this madness? Are you..?" she stopped herself. Mariya half-laughed and forced herself to her feet shakily. "That's it, isn't it? You're afraid of me. You're jealous that one day *I'll* rule."

A fire burned deep within Devon's eyes as he glared at his daughter, giving Mariya the confirmation she needed. He *was* jealous, and just as afraid. He had tried to hide it by covering it with haste and the want to kill her, but it was obvious. He still had strong connections to his once human self.

It all comes back to fear.

As many did, he feared the change that would come under Mariya's rule. She was the One, the chosen vampiress of legend, the harbinger of an age of hope and great growth. So Devon set about to kill her, the chosen.

Mariya carefully placed her hand over the gaping wound that slowly oozed thick crimson. Her hand dimly glowed with the energy she focused in the palm of her hand. With a wince, she pushed her hand *into* the wound and it started to heal, the bleeding stopping and a light scab soon formed.

She was dimly aware of the cautious energy from Esiviel, his wanting for her to get out of this place. With a sigh, she released the energy she had focused. Mutely, she shook her head and sent him a taste of her determination. Extreme fear hit her before she blocked the contact out of her mind. Biting her lip in anticipation, she unrolled the waistband of her skirt once, and a dagger fell into her palm. Then, everything was a blur.

Devon appeared behind her, trying to hit with a thrust, but Mariya turned at the last second to avoid the worst of the damage. As she planned, it barely grazed the surface and only a red line was visible from the fresh tear in her dress. With a quick prep step, she turned and slashed at her father and took advantage of the vulnerable position he left himself in. Her blade obediently carved a deep, red line through his flesh and he recoiled with a gasp.

The hate in his eyes grew darker, deeper, heavier alongside the crimson that now blossomed and spread across the white fabric of his tattered tunic. He pressed a hand over the wound, the red not stopping at his hands and oozing through his tightly clenched fingers like water through paper. Instead of the satisfaction Mariya had anticipated, regret rose in her stomach. She was torn; part of her screamed to finish it now and never have anyone, or anything, chase her again, while the other felt sorry for Devon.

After all, she thought for a second, *He is my father.*

Then the feelings again gave way to an intense hatred at the memories of the heinous crimes he committed, all because she glanced behind her at her mate that was barely hanging on. The victims, the blood, the darkness, the pain.

Everything.

The stare down soon ended when Devon nearly disappeared. He was too fast for Mariya to follow with her eyes, but she tried to rely on her sixth sense. As soon as she thought she got a hold on where he was, she felt a sharp pain spread up her back to the base of her neck. Then the onslaught continued. Each consecutive slash was faster than the previous one, bringing more pain. Each hit made her weaker, bringing her closer to the gate. But she fought it with everything she had left.

It all comes back to fear.

By the end of the assault, Mariya was on her knees, tightly clutching her locket as if memories long past could save her. As if forgotten pain could change the course of history, as if *they* would protect her from death.

Her silk dress was now rags, barely clinging to her

thin frame from the blood oozing out of the lacerations now covering her aching body. Taking a deep breath and holding it, she gave life one last fighting chance. Summoning all of her remaining energy and emotion, Mariya made a barrier around her. Just as the purple shield started to glint around her, she started to slip.

There were calls from the other side, trying to urge her on. Mariya weakly shook from the effort not to cry, trying to be resilient to the very bitter end. Her blood now covered the floor, mixing with that of the many nameless victims to create a sort of painted scenery for her final act. She was roughly aware of the healing energy that brushed her mind; but she blocked it out, only to hear Esiviel utter a curse at her in the corner. Mariya smiled at him the best she could, because she knew she couldn't go on like this. She knew it was over.

That she had failed.

Her father had won.

11. Dead

Devon stepped up, gasping and still covering his one wound with his now blood stained hand. "It's over, my dear," he grinned, watching Mariya let the barrier down and seem to give up. "Long live the queen." With a monstrous grin, he went to give the killing stroke.

But Mariya *wasn't* giving up.

Not like this.

Not that easily.

Then time seemed to freeze right there. It only just then occurred to Mariya that she didn't know exactly what she had been expecting for her death. But she knew that despite her fears and the years of running, that she hadn't been expecting this. Maybe she wanted something more dramatic, a Hollywood ending. She could have died in battle in some far off land, protecting her kin. One thing was for sure; anything, and anywhere, but this would have been so much better.

Bam!

Time caught up in a rush, knocking the remaining air out of Mariya. As she gasped, trying to calm herself back down, half a million images all flashed in her mind at speeds so fast they seemed to all melt together.

First feed.

First kiss.

Her oaths to Esiviel.

Her investiture as princess after her mother's death.

Mariya knew she *had* to do something, anything. Either way, her life as a half-vampire was done. She was at the crossroads of her life: full blood or death. Then the world faded away, nothing else mattered. It was Devon and herself, locked in the Daddy/Daughter Date Dance from Hell.

Damned if she did, damned if she didn't.

Mariya struggled to gather her remaining energy into a ball, and grip her dagger one last time. Biting her lip, she thrust her dagger into Devon's chest, just as his embedded itself in her shoulder. She drew in a gasp of pain, but blocked the feeling out and forced her blade in deeper.

Time froze again.

As quickly as it had stopped, it started again. Mariya felt a horrifying crunch ripple up her arm as her dagger pierced Devon's weakly beating heart. It pulsed just once before falling still, just as a bile rose in her throat. Swallowing harshly, she pulled his blade from her shoulder and let go of hers. Immediately following, her father stumbled back several steps, blood dripping from the corners of his mouth. More spurted from the gaping hole in his chest, as he gurgled incoherently at her. He fell over, and lay still were he landed, his face frozen in an expression of incomprehensive shock.

His blood soon joined hers on the dance floor, for the last waltz of the evening. Yet, Mariya couldn't bring herself to breathe the sigh of relief she had sought for so long. As she stood, her breath caught in her throat. She instantly fell to one knee, a red haze starting to fill her vision. Her anger finally wore off, and the pain began to take its overdue toll on her failing body. Yet she couldn't bring herself to cry. She had won.

It was over.

Epilogue

"Mariya!" Someone called to her far off in the distance, way beyond the light that now enveloped her. The sound of shattering chains soon followed.

That's right, she thought to herself drunkenly, *I fought my father for him. . .*

She weakly looked up at Esiviel, his silver eyes hazed over with tears. She smiled at him, her eyes fluttering shut, "Hey." Her grip loosened and she fell over, only to land in his arms. "You're hurt again. . ." she whispered lazily, as if she had just noticed his injuries. "Stupid. . .can't you take of yourself without. . . me. . ?"

"Shh. . ." Esiviel whispered shakily, smoothing down her hair.

His gentle shakes vibrated through her, but she paid them

no mind. She was barely there anymore, barely aware of the fact that she was in his arms. Mariya was at death's door, and crossing the threshold. Esiviel bit his lip nervously, cursing the moon and the eternal, blessed darkness of death. There was only one thing that could save her, but that would break their oaths.

Death or afterlife?

Darkness or eternal death?

"Mariya, my love, stay with me," he whispered, forcing back the tears that welled to the surface. "I need you to be tough. C'mon, hang on. For me."

Cursing every deity known to both vampires and man, he reopened one of the many cuts on his wrist. Thick, dark crimson slowly oozed to the surface, and he sighed sorrowfully. *Forgive me, Mariya.*

Taking a deep breath, Esiviel gently pressed his wrist to Mariya's lips. "Drink," he instructed her roughly, and she weakly obeyed.

It was the oddest sensation, for both of them. Mariya weakly gagged, recognizing the sour taste of his blood. Yet, he refused to pull away from her although pain now racked his usually numb body. It was as if the remaining bit of life left in him was being stolen away. But as her guardian, he couldn't let her die. Not here, not now.

Not ever.

After what seemed forever, Mariya fell silent. Her breathing suddenly became labored, then silenced just as quickly. Esiviel sighed sadly as he felt her heartbeat slow until

164

he could barely feel it anymore. Color drained from her skin, the warmth about her already dissipating. She looked calm and peaceful, although a new battle was raging inside her.

Mariya would never have to take another breath for the need to live. She would never again feel the sun on her face, she belonged to the dark now. She had officially joined the ranks of the undead, right here in this desecrated tomb of death and blood. The sun had set for her human existence, and gave way to the moon. Now was her beginning of her reign in the world of darkness. Forever.

Check mate.

Acknowledgments

Sarah, whose dare made this all possible. It was because of her that Mariya took shape to start with, and I am eternally grateful that she pushed me out of my age of being a fanfic writer.

And who am I kidding? My parents, who understood, or tried to, when I spent many nights during any vacation I got working on my computer. Despite losing sleep over this book from the first time I started writing, because Mariya and Esiviel refused to leave me alone, they stood beside me. Thank you *so* much.

Lauran Henderson, my best friend ever who helped me through hard parts with roleplay and even helping make characters when my brain refused to budge. Also, thanks for helping with the "threatening" element. You are my horror queen!

Any of my favorite authors, and the many bands on my playlist. These guys are the reason I never stopped writing. I am deeply grateful for all of my muses. Thanks for helping make my own breed of vampires.

And last not but least, my wonderful family that helped me gather enough money to make my dream come true. Because of you guys, Mariya isn't just a hazy vision on my computer but an actual book. I love and miss all of you, near and far. Brightest blessings.